MW01037481

JEM + TEAN: GUYS GONE WILD

SHORT STORIES FROM THE LAMB AND THE LION

GREGORY ASHE

H&B

This is a work of fiction. Names, characters, places, and incidents either are the
product of the author's imagination or are used fictitiously, and any resemblance to
actual persons, living or dead, business establishments, events, or locales is entirely
coincidental.

Jem + Tean: Guys Gone Wild
Copyright © 2021 Gregory Ashe

All rights reserved. No part of this book may be reproduced in any form, stored in
any retrieval system, or transmitted in any form by any means — electronic,
mechanical, photocopy, recording, or otherwise — without prior written permission
of the publisher, except as provided by United States of America copyright law. For
permission requests and all other inquiries, contact: contact@hodgkinandblount.com

Published by Hodgkin & Blount
https://www.hodgkinandblount.com/
contact@hodgkinandblount.com

Published 2021
Printed in the United States of America

Trade Paperback ISBN: 978-1-63621-013-1
eBook ISBN: 978-1-63621-012-4

FIRST DATES

This story takes place before *The Same Breath*.

1

Teancum Leon, who went by Tean, wasn't sure how he'd been talked into going on a blind date.

"You're going to like Derek," Hannah said as she pulled shirts from Tean's closet and threw them on the bed. Some of them landed on Scipio, Tean's dog. The black Lab shook them off and sprinted out of the room. Tean looked wistfully after him. "He's so smart, and I know you like smart guys. And he checks all your boxes: you don't work with him, he's not hung up on the whole Mormon thing, he's got a normal life and friends."

"He can't be that normal," Tean said, "not if he's still single."

"You're still single."

"That's my whole point."

Frowning, Hannah picked up a shirt. "Do you have any clothing that isn't brown?"

"Why would I?"

Hannah opened her mouth, paused, and closed it again. "Let's go shopping. We've got plenty of time."

Tean said no, and they agreed to disagree, which meant that Tean ended up at Nordstrom, pawing through the clearance racks and wincing at the price tags.

"That's a nice color," Hannah said, tucking chestnut hair behind her ears. "That would look great on you."

With a groan, Tean dropped it into her arms, where a pile was accumulating. "Can't I just go home, please? I'll call this guy and tell him I'm sick. I'll tell him I've got a parasite. A tapeworm. That always works. I'll tell him it's the kind that they have to pull out of your butt."

Hannah just hummed to herself as she flicked through the Medium section of another rack.

"People are fascinated by tapeworms," Tean said. "And rightly so. They can get up to eighty feet long coiled up inside your intestine."

"What about green?" Hannah said, holding up a shirt.

"They can live inside you for thirty years. That's longer than the average marriage. That means you're more likely to have a long-term, healthy relationship with a tapeworm than with another human being."

Hannah cocked her head, looking at the shirt, then at him, and then sighed and hung the shirt on the rack again. "Probably not lime green."

"Actually," Tean said, "I really think that's what I should do. I'm not feeling well anyway. I might have a fever."

"You don't have a fever."

"I just started to feel—"

Hannah pressed the back of a hand to his forehead, and she repeated, "You don't have a fever."

"A thermometer—"

But she had already glided away, still humming. Tean thought the tune was "Onward Christian Soldiers."

At the checkout register, the clerk was a young woman in braces.

"They're glow in the dark rubber bands," she told Tean when she noticed him noticing. "My boyfriend likes them."

"That's so cute," Hannah said. "Isn't that cute?"

"You should chew some of those plaque disclosing tablets next time," Tean said. "Before he kisses you. Maybe he'd like that too."

The girl wrinkled her nose.

"Go wait in the car," Hannah said.

"I was trying to be helpful."

"No, you weren't. And give me your credit card, please."

It was a spring day in the Salt Lake Valley, which meant perfection. The sun was warm, the mountain breeze brisk, the sky the same blue as deep glacial ice. The only off note was the smell of construction: diesel exhaust, freshly rolled asphalt, and hot metal. Tean sat on the bumper of Hannah's car; two rows over, a young man and a young woman were making out, pressed up against a RAV4. The young woman was taking the initiative; she had the young man pressed up against a door, and every once in a while he'd whimper and slap the RAV4 like he was starring in a bad porno. Well, just a regular porno, probably. Not that Tean had much experience with that. All that slapping couldn't be good for the door, though. If they got going any harder, they'd need a plunger to get the dents out.

"Aww," Hannah said, following his gaze.

"It's like that scene from *Alien*," Tean said. "Only in reverse, I guess."

"What scene?"

Tean sighed and shook his head. When Hannah held out a bag of clothes, he accepted it. "Is there a tracking collar in here too? Or are you going to class things up and embed an RFID chip at the back of my neck before you turn me loose?"

"That's funny," Hannah said as they got in the car. "You should try to be funny like that on your date tonight. Derek likes funny guys."

"I could show him that weird mole, the one that's probably cancerous. It's funny looking."

"That's not what I mean."

"I think I'll just call him and be sick. I think that'll be the best thing for everyone. I think that's a really great idea."

"No."

Tean leaned forward, elbows on knees, blinking out at the glitter of glass—windows, windshields, all of it flashing with the sun high over the valley. "I could just go home. I'll walk Scipio. I'll eat some of those scrambled eggs I burned last night."

"How did you manage to burn scrambled eggs?"

"And then I'll just turn off all the lights."

"Wait. Hold on. You burned the eggs and you still kept them?"

"And then I'll just sit there. It'll be perfectly, blessedly dark, and I'll just stare at a blank wall, and I'll contemplate the pure, cosmic horror of existence. And maybe I'll rent a movie."

"No."

"There's this YouTube channel with nine hours of screaming."

"No."

"You just click play, and it's like listening to the damned in hell."

Hannah just shook her head. "Honestly, sometimes I think you don't even want to find somebody to date."

"Lots of variety, you know? That's what makes it so good. Not just high-pitched shrieks over and over again. There's this one guy who's got a really deep voice. Around hour seven and a half, it sounds like he gets in a car crash."

"Derek has a really deep voice."

Tean covered his eyes with both hands.

Before too long, they were turning into Tean's apartment complex, Hannah pulling the car into one of the guest spots. She turned off the engine and said, "What are you going to do about your hair?"

"It's hair. It's on my head. I'm already doing better than like sixty percent of guys."

"Gosh," Hannah said. "I loved frosted tips. Do you think frosted tips are back in?"

"Goodbye."

"I bet we could finish the tips before you have to meet Derek."

Tean opened the door.

"Now," Hannah said, "I don't want to go all mama bear on you, but I know it's been a long time, so don't get swept off your feet. If you get lucky, be sure to use protection—"

Tean launched himself out of the car.

Hannah's shouting followed him: "Wear the blue shirt. Derek loves blue!"

Lugging the bag toward the stairs, Tean tried to be positive. Maybe tonight wouldn't be so bad. Maybe he would, to borrow Hannah's term, get lucky. Maybe he'd stick himself with a pin from one of the new shirts, and it would have flesh-eating bacteria on it. Hope springs eternal.

2

Jeremiah Berger, who went by Jem, wasn't sure how he'd been talked into going on a blind date.

"Is he rich?" Jem asked. He was moving around the apartment where he squatted, giving everything a once-over: the single mattress on the floor, a dirty sheet tucked under the corners to hold it in place, and a blanket balled up at one end; dirty clothes in one corner, clean clothes in another; two extension cords running in from the window (he paid the downstairs neighbors twenty bucks a week for power), with one of the cords going to a fan, and the other snaking out of the bedroom and into the kitchen, where it connected to the refrigerator. He thought about changing the sheets, and then he didn't. He kicked the dirty clothes into the closet and shut the door. Like a gentleman.

"I mean," Tinajas said, her muscular arms crossed over her chest, "he's definitely higher up the ladder than you."

"You don't have to be mean about it."

"You missed some underwear."

Jem grinned, retrieved the pink briefs from where they were partially hidden by the mattress, and tossed them in the closet. "Not mine."

"Gross."

"I think his name was Todd."

"Extra gross."

"What's wrong with the name Todd?"

"The fact that you don't even know his name, dumbass."

"Grow up," Jem said. "It's the twenty-first century. Anonymous hookups are the new going steady."

"I'll remember that next time you're filling a scrip for penicillin."

Jem's grin grew. "But seriously, is he rich? Like, not the annoying kind of rich where it's all locked up in a trust fund or they use credit cards and think it's funny to wear thrift-store clothes."

"He has a name."

"Todd?"

Tinajas's dark eyes narrowed.

"Ok, ok. Um. I know you told me. It was something super Mormon-y. Bristol."

"You're unbearable when you think you're cute. What prompted this? Was it finding that underwear? Did that make you feel annoyingly self-confident?"

"Brie."

"He's a boy. A cute boy. A sweet boy. He's not a European city or a cheese. And I'm deeply regretting setting him up with you."

"Brigham."

Tinajas rolled her eyes.

"Am I right?"

"Yes."

"And Brigham is going to be super rich, like, flashing a forty-thousand-dollar Rolex that I can get off his dresser after I bang him to Boystown, right?"

"Brigham is twenty-four years old, and he just came out to his parents, and he's sweet and innocent, and as I go on listing his qualities, I realize you are totally wrong for him."

"Hey!"

"I'll call him and cancel."

"Hold on, hold on." Jem folded his arms. "He doesn't have to be rich."

"No, this was a mistake."

"You said he was cute. Is he cute? Really?"

"Look, Jem, I love you. Kind of. But Brigham is a starry-eyed baby, and I don't want him to be another one of your marks."

"Just wait a second. Just wait one second. I'm offended. I'm really offended."

"You're trying to flex your biceps is what you're doing."

"I can be a really sweet guy too."

"You were literally just talking about 'banging him to Boystown' and stealing his watch."

When Tinajas moved toward the door, Jem threw himself into the doorway, his body making an X. "I can be sweet and also have a backup plan."

"You're too old for him."

"You said he's, what, twenty-four? That's only three years. That's nothing."

"That's not what I meant," Tinajas said, and her dark eyes were sad.

"Look, I promise I'll behave. I'll cut up his food for him and make sure he eats his vegetables, and if he's really good, I'll buy him an ice cream cone at the end of the night."

"Why?"

"You just said—"

"No, you didn't even want to go on this date. Now you're desperate."

Jem drew himself up to his full height, trying on his best martyred expression. "It's the principle of the thing. I'm not going to stand around while you make me sound like some sort of scamster fuckboy."

"I caught you selling fake Ray Bans on a blanket outside my office last week."

"Those glasses were awesome!"

"Also, you have no principles."

Jem opened his mouth, but then a knock came at the door. He froze.

Tinajas, who never missed anything, fixed him with her gaze. "Who's that?"

"Nobody."

"Really? Nobody just knocked at your front door?"

"You know what? I think you're right. I think you should go, and we can continue this conversation over the phone when you're—no, go that way, you have to leave by the window, oof."

The last was the sound he made when she elbowed him in the gut.

Jem was still catching his breath as she marched toward the door and opened it. When she saw the man in the hall, she planted her hands on her hips and looked up at him. Kike was holding a bottle of Mad Dog, and his dark eyes widened as he looked past Tinajas to Jem. Jem just shrugged and held up his hands.

"You're kidding," Tinajas said. She turned to Jem. "You're kidding me, right?"

"It's not what it looks like."

"It looks like you're hooking up with my degenerate coworker a few hours before you have a date."

"This is strictly, um—"

"A courtesy call," Kike offered.

Tinajas spun away to point a finger at Kike. He flinched; Jem noticed that he was free-balling it in his joggers.

"That's right," Jem said. "We each provide a valuable service—"

"You're going to hell," Tinajas said. "I don't even believe in hell, but you're going there. Just you. And you're going to be there alone." She pushed past Kike and strode down the hall.

Jem wiggled out into the hall after her and called, "So Brigham and I, we're still on, right? Tinajas? Tin? I will be a perfect gentleman!"

Kike was already shucking his clothes in the doorway, and he grabbed Jem's shirt and dragged him into the apartment.

"I've only got twenty minutes," Kike said.

"Fuck me," Jem said as he struggled out of his shirt. "I'm going to hell."

3

The texts with Derek had been heating up all afternoon.

god ur cute. wanna dick pic?

Maybe a headshot first? Tean realized the moment he hit send that he'd made a poor choice of words.

Sure enough, a close-up dick pic zoomed into his inbox a moment later.

cum on, now u

Checking the mirror, Tean immediately gave up on his hair, which was brushed back and bushy. On good days, Hannah called it a mane, but not in a positive way. He would have been happy with fixing his eyebrows, but no matter how many times he tried, he couldn't get them to not look any less huge and bristling. He caught his glasses, which had a broken frame, right before they slid off his nose, and then he gave up and took a picture of his face and sent it.

playing hard to get. daddy like

Tean just let that one float.

let me see ur hole, Derek texted after a minute had passed.

That's second-date material, I think.

A series of laughing emojis followed. *seriously, though, are we going to bone tonight*

Tean put the phone down. He went out onto the balcony, with Scipio trailing after him, the Lab nuzzling into his hand and rocking his weight into Tean's leg. He could see the Wasatch Mountains from here; the day was so bright that it bleached the sky, shining hard against the bare stone peaks.

When he went back inside, Derek had texted again: *cuz I'm missing a night with my boys for this*

Tean considered taking a screenshot and sending it to Hannah. He was trying to remember how Hannah claimed to know him. Trying to remember if she'd told him something that would explain this—I got his number off of a bathroom stall, something like that.

Instead, he texted back, *I guess we'll see where the night takes us.*

boi, I'm gonna get up in that tight pussy and fuck u so hard ur insides are gonna be mush

To be fair, it had been a long time since Tean had gone on a date. He vaguely remembered that being honest and polite was the best approach, so he said: *Look, Hannah says you're a great guy, and I'm looking forward to meeting you, but I think this is moving too fast for me. Can we just get dinner and have a nice time?*

The text bubble that signaled someone composing a message appeared, disappeared, and then appeared again. It went on for a distressingly long time; sweat was prickling under Tean's arms when the message finally arrived.

Yeah, of course. I'm really sorry. Sometimes I overcompensate trying to play the game. I hope I didn't offend you.

Smiling, Tean typed back, *Thanks for understanding. I'll see you in a couple of hours?*

Actually, could you pick me up? I'm having car trouble. I was going to have my friend drive me, but you seem really sweet.

Of course.

An address came through a moment later.

Two hours later, Tean drove across town. The address Derek had provided took him from his Central City apartment east toward Emigration Canyon, cutting south into an older neighborhood before he reached the mountains. The houses here dated from the fifties, small and boxy, some with narrow wood siding, some with wide slabs of asbestos, all of them with their paint peeling. When Tean parked, he found himself sitting in front of a tiny home. It had a hint of a furnace vent behind the sagging roofline, aluminum awnings over the windows, and a lithograph of Jesus taped in the front window. The car in the driveway was an ancient BMW, as boxy as the house, with leper-spots of rust across the roof and trunk.

No wonder Derek was having car troubles, Tean thought as he unbuckled himself and made his way up to the door.

When he knocked, he could hear voices on the other side of the door. TV voices, he realized after a moment. Then a slow, dragging noise that he connected, after a moment, to footsteps. A chain rattled, a bolt flipped back, and the door swung open.

The man standing behind the door looked like he wouldn't see ninety again, his skin tight in places, loose in others, gray and slightly translucent. He had a thick head of white hair, and he stared out at Tean from behind enormous bifocals, his eyes bright.

"Yes?" The word was softly accented. German, Tean thought. Or maybe a Scandinavian country. "Hello?"

"Hi," Tean said. "I'm here to pick up Derek."

The old man stared, unblinking, and sweat gathered at Tean's hairline. He shoved his glasses up before they had the chance to fall off his face.

"Mama," the man called over his shoulder, followed by a string of words in what Tean was increasingly sure was German. More steps moved inside the house, and Tean threw a look over his shoulder, staring at his truck longingly.

Then the door swung open wider, and a woman who had to have been as old as the man stood there, her hair dyed pink and brushed into a faux hawk. She was wearing a cardigan, and she played with the mother-of-pearl buttons as she contemplated Tean.

When the man had finished speaking, the woman nodded, reached out, and grabbed Tean's arm. Her grip was surprisingly strong. "You come inside now. We will find your Derek."

"Oh, no, I don't—"

But Tean was already being towed into the house, the air smelling like fried sausages, all the curtains closed, the door shuttering the last of the light as it closed behind him. The interior illumination consisted exclusively of Dresden porcelain lamps, primarily shepherdesses, placed around the room in strange pairings. A plaid sofa and a television dominated the front room; on the TV, *Modern Family* was playing.

"Sit, sit, sit, sit, sit," the old man was saying, taking over as Tean's warden and steering him toward the sofa while the woman tottered through an opening that connected, from what Tean could see, into the kitchen.

"I really need to go," Tean said, but he found himself sitting anyway, and then the old man was settling onto the other end of the sofa. "I think there was a mistake—"

"What is his last name, this Derek?" the woman asked from the opening. She was holding a stapled packet, probably a church directory.

"I don't know."

"But he told you this house?"

Tean shrugged and nodded.

"We will find him," the woman announced, opening the packet to its first page and dialing a number on an ancient, wall-mounted landline. "Brother Anderson? Yes, hello. This is a very important call."

Covering his face, Tean rested his elbows on his knees. She was going to call everyone in the directory. "I should go."

"Papa," the woman said, "he is a guest."

"It is very nice to have you," the old man said, standing with what looked like a great deal of difficulty. "It is very nice to have a guest."

He shuffled toward the kitchen, and Tean uncovered his face. This was his chance to escape. But as he scooted to the edge of the sofa cushion, he thought of the excitement in the old man's eyes when he had answered the door, he thought of the quaver in his voice when he said, *It is very nice to have a guest.*

Tean sat back on the sofa; it wasn't like he had anywhere better to go.

The old man came back with slow, careful steps, balancing a plate with a pastry.

"You really don't have to—" Tean said.

But the old man waved him to silence, taking his time setting up a TV tray, arranging the plate and fork neatly.

"Papa, give him some of the juice."

"Juice," Papa said to Tean.

"No, I'm really fine—"

But it didn't matter, because the juice came anyway, and Mama was still calling in the C's—"Yes, hello, Sister Carmichael, this is a very important phone call"—and then Papa eased his weight onto the sofa next to Tean.

"It's very good," Tean said after a few bites of pastry.

Papa smiled and patted his shoulder.

"You really don't know anyone named Derek?" Tean asked.

Papa shook his head. Then he picked up an ancient, chunky remote and aimed it at the TV. "Do you know this show?"

"I've seen a few episodes. I mostly watch botched surgeries on YouTube. I mean, when I have time for TV."

Papa nodded along as Tean spoke, and when Tean had finished, he said, "This one is Claire, and she is the mother. She is very —" He said a word in German and made a fist. "They will all wear white pants to the family picture."

In spite of himself, Tean smiled. "Sounds like they're going to have problems."

Papa patted his shoulder again, and his voice was soft and slightly confused as he said, "It is very good of you to come."

4

Leatherby's was a creamery that also doubled as a diner. The burgers were good. The cones, shakes, and sundaes were out of this world. Jem had gone there plenty of times, but never on a first date. As he pushed through the door, the smell of fresh waffles hit him. Young families crowded the tables and booths. He wondered if he'd made a mistake.

He'd barely scanned half the room before he saw Brigham standing halfway out of his chair, waving frantically. Jem sighed and considered a quick retreat—or, if things got messy, faking a seizure. Then he made his way across the restaurant. Brigham looked young, the way so many Mormon guys did—a kind of extended adolescence that was probably partly social, partly genetic, and partly lifestyle. He had short, dark hair that was heavily gelled, acne along his jawline, and a huge, wobbly smile. The robin's-egg blue polo and the cargo shorts made him look seventeen, tops. A very nerdy seventeen.

"Jem?" Brigham said, the word exploding out of him before Jem had reached the table. "Oh my gosh, it's so nice to meet you." He came around the table, got caught in the legs of his own chair, stumbled, and fell into Jem's arms.

Laughing, Jem helped him get his footing. "Hi. Brigham, right?"

"Oh frick," Brigham said. "Oh frick."

"It's ok. Take two. Hi. You must be Brigham."

He smiled. "Yep. You must be Jem." Then he pulled Jem into a huge bro hug, pounding his back.

Jem was laughing again when he managed to get free. He gestured to the table, and they sat. At the table behind Brigham, an older couple was watching them. When they saw Jem looking back at them, the man dropped his silverware and began to search for it on the ground, and the woman held a menu up in front of her face. Homophobes, probably, but at least they were ashamed to be busted for it.

The small talk started off really, really small. Jem asked about his day. Brigham described it in a blow-by-blow so thorough that Jem was actually kind of relieved—he turned his brain off and studied the menu, making noises to show he was listening.

"—and then at two-thirty I wanted to play Xbox, but I couldn't find *Destiny 2* because Mom had been cleaning up again even though I told her not to—" Brigham underscored this with a huge roll of his eyes and a grin.

That went on for a while until, at the table behind them, the man coughed loudly, and the woman banged the saltshaker on the table twice.

"—and Mom and Dad told me pleated khakis were a great choice for a first date—" Brigham flinched, licked his lips, and his eyes roved wildly. After a moment, he said, "What about you? How was your day?"

"Good," Jem said. "Busy."

"I bet," Brigham said, zipping up to a hundred again. "My dad is the hardest working guy I know, and—"

Two more claps of the saltshaker.

More wild-eyed staring, as though Brigham were searching the room for cue cards. "Oh, yeah," he said after a minute. "What do you do for work?"

"Day trading," Jem said, because he'd watched an episode of *Suits* the night before and he liked how the phrase sounded.

"That's so impressive," Brigham shouted. And then he was off again, talking about crowd control and DPS and other things Jem didn't understand at all.

No problem. Back to the menu. The patty melt sounded good, Jem thought. And definitely—oh.

"Holy shit," Jem said.

"—Mom was ironing my . . . um, are you ok?"

"Look at this." Jem held out the menu and tapped one of the desserts.

"Cookie Monster 'Me-Want-Cookie' Cookie Sundae," Brigham read. "Do you think they're allowed to use Cookie Monster?"

"Yeah, sure, but holy shit, Brigham, read the description: cookie dough ice cream on a six-inch, hot chocolate chip cookie with toasted cookie crumbs on top. And M&Ms. Doesn't that sound good?"

"It sounds like a lot of sugar," Brigham said doubtfully. "Mom said I had to get a single-scoop cone."

"Damn."

"And, um, I'd really," Brigham threw a single glance over his shoulder. "I'd really appreciate it if you didn't use that kind of language. I mean, you're so cute, and I think you're a great guy."

"You do?"

"Oh yeah. You're amazing. Such a good person."

"I am?"

"Yeah, I mean . . ." Brigham seemed to be looking for evidence and settled for: "You really are."

A second, lightning-fast glance over his shoulder.

"Tell you what," Jem said, raising his voice slightly. "These tables would fit together really easily. Mom, Dad, why don't you pull yours over and join us."

The man at the table behind them knocked his silverware off the table again. The woman's menu shot up again, shielding her face.

"Oh my gosh," Brigham moaned.

"If that's ok with you," Jem said to him.

"Oh frick. Oh frick. Oh frick."

"Brigham," Jem said with a smile, "relax. You seem really nice, and I think it'd make you more comfortable if they sat with us."

"This is so embarrassing," Brigham whispered.

"Not at all," Jem said. "What do you want to do?"

After a moment, Brigham nodded.

"Help me turn the table," Jem said, "and we'll get everybody settled."

Dinner with Mom and Dad actually turned out to be slightly less awkward than dinner with Mom and Dad pulling the conversational strings from the next table. Brigham relaxed—a lot—and Jem could see why: his parents did everything for him. His dad, who was balding and wearing a polo that was almost identical to Brigham's, made a few gruff comments and shook Jem's hand. His mom talked twice as fast and twice as much as Brigham. She talked exclusively about Brigham. She seemed determined to convey the wonders of Brigham in exhaustive detail.

"And he just finished a very difficult quest with his adventuring band," she said, reaching over Jem's arm to grab his silverware. She unrolled the utensils, unfolded the napkin, and spread it across Jem's lap. "The Xbox made this little beeping noise. It's quite the accomplishment."

"Mom," Brigham groaned. "It's not a quest. It's a mission."

"Well, I'm sorry, dear. On the last game they were all quests."

"And it's not an adventuring band. We're just a group." He smiled shyly at Jem. "It's a temporary alliance."

Mom ran the show after that. She directed both Brigham and Dad to a narrowing set of options on the menu, and she even gave Jem a few hard nudges toward the salads. He ignored her, of course, and ordered the patty melt. When the food came, Mom cut up Brigham's chicken tenders, and she made Dad eat the tomatoes he'd pushed to the side of his plate. Jem watched it all and wondered if this was what he'd been missing out on. It confirmed, more or less, what he'd pretty much already known: he hadn't been missing out on anything.

"Jem, sweetheart," Mom said, "if you save the second half of your sandwich, you can have it for lunch tomorrow."

Jem smiled at her and took a huge bite.

Mom was a stickler about dessert: Brigham and his parents each got a single-scoop cone.

"That's just so much sugar, Jem, dear. I really don't think—"

Jem ordered the Cookie Monster 'Me-Want-Cookie' Cookie Sundae before she had finished explaining; he heard kilocalories about eighteen times, but the rest was a meaningless buzz.

Toward the end of the night, when Mom was checking the foam clamshell containers, making sure Brigham and Dad had correctly packed up their half-dinners, a cold, dark tide rose in Jem. This was it, he guessed. This was what families were like. He'd known that, of course, but sometimes the reality of it came rushing in like tonight, threatening to drown him.

The check came, and Jem thought about the two stolen credit cards in his wallet that hadn't been canceled yet, and the cash he'd brought along just in case. Then he glanced at Dad, who was picking at a speck of dried ketchup on his polo, and remembered the magic words.

"Dad," Jem said, his voice serious, manly, all business, "I don't want any arguing about this. I am absolutely paying for dinner."

5

Tean was stepping out of his apartment when Hannah came up the stairs.

She froze when she saw him. Then she tucked her hair behind her ears and tried to smile.

"Hi," Tean said, adjusting the gear bag on his shoulder.

"Hi."

"I'm just—"

"You weren't answering your phone, and I was worried Derek had chopped you up in a bathtub."

"Look at me," Tean said. "Not chopped up at all. I've got to help Mrs. Wish."

"I'll come with you."

"Sure."

Mrs. Wish lived at the other end of the building, so they walked down the exterior corridor together. It was another of those perfect Utah spring days. In the shadowed corridor, it might have even been a little too cool, the air smelling like the damp indoor-outdoor carpeting. Mixed with the sound of Tean's and Hannah's steps came the thrum of tires, a boy singing "Put a Ring on It," a window thudding shut.

When Tean knocked, Mrs. Wish opened the door in a full-length nightgown, even though it was mid-afternoon, over which she'd thrown a terrycloth robe the color of Pepto-Bismol. Her long, white hair was up in a severe bun. An orangish tabby squirmed between her legs, obviously intending to make a break for it, but Mrs. Wish caught him by the scruff and pulled him into a hug.

"No, no, no, Senator Norris. Not today. Well, come in, unless you want the others to get bad ideas."

Tean nodded for Hannah to precede him into the house; she'd come with him once before, when Mrs. Wish had declared a state of emergency, and the two women exchanged smiles and murmured greetings. Tean followed, shutting the door behind him. He was immediately overwhelmed by the smell of animal dander, wet cat food, and the sickeningly sweet, floral potpourri that Mrs. Wish kept in collectible presidential ashtrays around the apartment. More than once Tean had been summoned to deal with a case of potpourri poisoning, when Mrs. Wish was convinced one of the Irreconcilables had overindulged when she wasn't looking.

"Senator Henry Cabot Lodge is in the guest room," Mrs. Wish said, pointing. "I've already put the bath towels in there."

Tean nodded.

"Violet will be by in an hour," Mrs. Wish said, setting Senator Norris back on the ground and then straightening to examine Tean. "Really, Dr. Leon, you could have at least made an effort."

"Mrs. Wish."

"I know, I know. You're not getting any younger, though. For that matter, neither is she. And she's a perfectly lovely girl. You could get her buckteeth fixed right up, and—"

"Mrs. Wish."

"Have it your way."

Nudging Hannah down the short hallway toward the bedrooms, Tean tried to navigate a path through the herd of cats. The exact number of animals in the apartment fluctuated between twelve and eighteen; Tean tried to count as they made their way through the space, but he came up with a different number every time, and after a while he gave up. Then a cat hissed, and Tean looked down in time to see a Sphynx sprinting toward the sofa. Hannah stared after the cat, her face horrified, one foot half-lifted from the ground. Mrs. Wish had her hands on her hips, glaring at them.

"I'm so sorry," Hannah said, glancing at Tean for help.

"La Follette," he offered.

"Mr. La Follette," Hannah said, "I didn't see you there. I'm really sorry."

"Well," Mrs. Wish said, scooping up the Sphynx and cradling him. "Really. He is a senator."

"Right," Hannah said. "Mr. Senator."

Mrs. Wish's whole body stiffened.

"You're making it worse," Tean whispered, catching her elbow and tugging her down the hall.

The guest room was, as far as Tean could tell, an entirely theoretical space. In the years that he had lived in the building, he'd never known Mrs. Wish to have a guest stay the night. Her children and grandchildren came for brief visits of varying frequency, but no one, as far as Tean could tell, had ever slept in this room.

He understood why. It reminded him of a pink birthday cake: a white poster bed with a pink canopy, a white duvet turned down to reveal satiny pink sheets, white furniture up against pink walls. And lace. A frothy ocean's worth of lace. The potpourri smell lingered— as well as the wet cat food smell and the dander—but this room had a charming accent note of mothballs. Mrs. Wish trailed after them, and Tean gave her an apologetic smile and closed the door before she—or any of the Irreconcilables—could join them.

Grabbing the bath towels that sat at the foot of the bed, Tean handed one to Hannah, and they spread them out on either side of the bed. He took treats from his gear bag, handed half to Hannah, and set some on the towel. He put out a couple of catnip toys, and then he got the lidocaine injection ready and laid it next to the sterilized suture kit. He could see spots of blood on the carpet and dust ruffle where Senator Henry Cabot Lodge had retreated.

"That bad, huh?" Hannah asked.

"Well, he is a senator. You could at least call him by his title."

A tiny smile flitted across Hannah's face. "You know what I mean."

Tean shrugged. "No second date. That's ok. I appreciate you wanting to help me find someone."

"What did he do?"

"Nothing."

"He's a second cousin, and I'll see him at the next family reunion. So you need to give me at least the degree of magnitude: am I going to kick his butt, or am I going to put sugar in his gas tank and then kick his butt?"

In spite of himself, Tean grinned, but he shook his head. "We just had different expectations, I think."

"Tean, I'm really sorry."

"It's ok. I still had a nice night."

The dust ruffle twitched. A pink nose and whiskers emerged, testing the air.

"Do you want me to keep trying?" Hannah said. "Do you want me to stop? You look so sad I feel like I'm going to break into a million pieces. Tell me what I can do."

"I'm fine," Tean said. "I'm just a little disappointed because I found out that YouTube video I like is really just a compilation of those screaming goats." He shook his head. "The hours I've wasted."

"Please tell me you did not talk to Derek about the cosmic joke of existence or go on a rant about how humanity's only genuine form of communication is howling into the abyss."

Tean watched Senator Henry Cabot Lodge creep out from under the bed.

"Please tell me you did not make him listen to those goat screams on YouTube."

"Give me a little credit, Hannah."

"Thank God. I honestly don't know what I would have told Great-Grandma."

"That's second-date stuff."

Hannah groaned.

Senator Henry Cabot Lodge had a nasty gash along his flank, probably from fighting with Senator Poindexter, a nasty Siamese who tended to start all the scrapping that took place among the Irreconcilables. Lodge, a beautiful Persian, came closer, sniffing once at Tean and then investigating the treats. Tean leaned forward, took the edges of the towel, and in a few careful movements swaddled the Persian in spite of the poor senator's yowling protests.

First, he cleaned the wound and examined it. Hannah helped to keep the senator swaddled. Then he administered the lidocaine injection. Then he stitched the gash—it was a borderline case, but he knew Mrs. Wish wouldn't let him leave without doing everything he could. When he'd finished and cleaned up, he accepted the swaddled senator from Hannah and left the guest room. Mrs. Wish was perched on the sofa, crying softly into a handkerchief.

"The patient is going to make a full recovery," Tean said, passing over Senator Henry Cabot Lodge. "But you'll want to keep him away from the others for a few days—maybe keep Senator Poindexter away for even longer."

"Thank you," Mrs. Wish said, holding the Persian gingerly and dabbing at her eyes. "That was a very gentlemanly thing to do, Dr. Leon."

"My pleasure."

"I'll send Violet over with some hot cross buns."

"You don't need to do that."

"Of course I do. And," her voice was gaining strength, "you could at least have the decency to make an advance on the poor girl. It's not her fault she's got that crooked eye."

Hannah was trying not to laugh as they left.

"Does she know that you're—"

"Of course. She just doesn't care."

Hannah looped her arm through his. "You know what you need, Dr. Leon?"

"What, Dr. Prince?"

"You need to find a good guy."

6

The next night, Jem was working with Sammi. She was only sixteen, and she looked even younger, but she was already turning into a pro. They picked City Creek because the newly developed shopping mall drew high-end customers. For about half an hour, Jem wandered the mall, enjoying the air cooling against his skin, the murmur of the creek that ran over pale stone, the smell of pretzels, the movement of bodies. In the early evening, the mall was busy; it had become a kind of shopping paradise, and people came just to walk and kill some time.

Adjusting his glasses—a fake pair held together with a single drop of Elmer's—Jem spotted the sheep: a middle-aged man carrying

JEM + TEAN: GUYS GONE WILD

some extra pounds, with a much younger woman clinging to him. The man was red-faced, and the candy-cane-striped shirt just made it worse; the girl on his arm had thin blond hair and sleepy eyes. Sammi was twenty yards ahead, dipping her feet in the creek, occasionally talking to a boy who had approached her but clearly didn't know what to say. When Sammi glanced over, Jem caught her eye and pointed out the sheep. Sammi nodded, turned to the boy, and began talking: big smile, big gestures. The boy melted.

The next part was all about timing. Jem began to move toward the sheep, while Sammi and the boy sprinted in the opposite direction. Jem couldn't tell if they were racing or playing tag. Or maybe something else, some other game Sammi had chosen. The boy was grinning, obviously holding back, letting Sammi pull ahead.

The middle-aged man and his much younger girlfriend stopped at a storefront, staring through the window.

The man said something, pointing to something on the other side of the window.

"Oh my gosh, Wilson," the girl said in a dead voice, smacking her gum. "It's really cool."

They talked like that for a few more minutes before turning and walking again.

Sammi was sprinting full speed now, coming up behind them.

Jem quickened his pace.

Timing; it was all timing.

At the same moment that Jem stepped in front of the man — Wilson — Sammi ran into both Wilson and his girlfriend from behind. The couple stumbled forward. The girlfriend squealed. Wilson swore. But they couldn't stop themselves: they crashed into Jem, and he rocked backward. The glasses flew from his face, and when they struck the ground, the single bead of Elmer's glue gave out. The bridge split.

As Wilson caught his girlfriend and steadied her, Sammi and the boy raced away, both of them laughing.

"Get back here," Wilson shouted after them. "Get back here and apologize!"

"What the shit?" Jem said, turning on Wilson. "Watch where you're going, buddy!"

"It was those kids," Wilson said.

"Yeah," the girlfriend said in a dead voice. "Those kids."

"Where are my glasses?" Jem said. Wilson and the girlfriend looked around automatically, and Jem waited for them to spot the glasses first. The girlfriend jabbed an index finger toward the broken halves. "You broke my glasses," Jem shouted, "you dumb fuck!"

"Hey," Wilson said. "Listen, it's not my fault—"

"Do you have any idea how much these cost?" Jem gathered the broken glasses and held them out in display. "These are Louis Vuitton's, dumbass. They cost more than your fucking car."

"Watch your language," Wilson said, his face getting even redder. "There's a lady—"

"Security," Jem shouted. "Somebody get security. I want this on record for when I sue the shit out of you."

Wilson looked a little waxy under the red mottling his cheeks. The girlfriend's eyes didn't look quite as sleepy anymore.

"Hey," Wilson said. "Hold on. There's no need—I mean, I didn't even—"

"Witnesses, asshole," Jem said. "There's a hundred people that just saw you crash into me and break my glasses."

Wilson and the girl traded looks. "Ok, but, there's no need to file a report," Wilson finally said. "And there's no reason we can't just figure this out on our own."

After that, it was just haggling, and Jem was good at haggling. When it was all done, he gave Sammi her cut and offered her a ride back to the apartment.

"I'm gonna hang out for a while," she said, looking at the boy. Jem looked too, and the poor kid blushed bright red.

"Don't do anything I wouldn't do," Jem said.

Sammi rolled her eyes.

"Or most of the stuff I would do," Jem said. "Don't do that either."

Flipping Jem off, Sammi ran to join the boy.

Jem rode home on his Kawasaki. He climbed the fire escape, let himself in through the window, and kicked off his sneakers. When he checked his phone, he had a message from Kike.

Want some company ;-)

Jem texted back a thumbs-up.

Twenty minutes later, Jem had showered and Kike was knocking at the door. He let him in, and they hit the ground running: kissing, stripping each other out of their clothes, and then a quick, hard fuck.

When they'd finished, they lay tangled together on the mattress. After a few minutes, Jem ran fingers through Kike's hair, enjoying the texture of the coarse curls, the slight woodsy scent to whatever Kike used to style it.

Laughing, Kike wiggled free.

"Where do you think you're going?" Jem said.

"Shower," Kike said.

"Wait a couple of minutes. I was all warm and comfy."

Kike shook his head. "You really don't get how this works, do you?" He reached back, touched himself, and winced. "God, you are a fucking jackhammer sometimes."

"Let me make it up to you," Jem said, patting the mattress.

"You're so lame," Kike said. Standing, he added, "Roll us some joints, will you?"

He padded away. From the bathroom came the hiss of water. Jem stared up at the cracked plaster ceiling. Closed his eyes. He felt hot and flushed in patches, and he rolled his head to the side, scrubbing his face against the mattress. When the water cut off and the shower curtain rings jangled, he was staring up at the ceiling again.

Wet footsteps. "Did you roll those joints?"

"Not yet."

Kike dressed—he was obviously planning on going out, clubbing or a party or another hookup, because he took a lot of time checking and double-checking himself in the bathroom. Jem threw on sweatshorts and a zip-up hoodie. They climbed out onto the fire escape and lit up, the embers of the joints flaring against the backdrop of the valley's lights. When the weed finally started hitting, Jem sagged against the building's bricks: sharp edges, lingering warmth from the sunny day.

"Come on," Kike said. "Don't be like this."

"Like what?"

"We had fun, right?"

"Sure."

"Well, that's ok, right?"

"Sure."

Before speaking again, Kike took a long drag on the joint. The smoke, when he exhaled, was just more darkness, a veil of it drifting between them and then gone.

"You're cute when you pout," Kike said, kissing Jem on the cheek and then getting to his feet.

"Fuck off."

Laughing, Kike ruffled Jem's hair. He killed the joint and flicked the butt over the rail. "You know what you need?"

Tonight, the weed was making Jem dizzy, and he let his head fall back. The stars spun overhead. "A date with mom and dad and their baby boy, apparently."

"You need to find a nice guy."

CHEAP SEATS
This story takes place before *The Same Place*.

1

"It's probably going to be sold out."

Jem nodded and tried not to smile, quickening his pace.

Tean, alternating between a jog and a fast walk as he tried to keep up with Jem, shoved his hair back with both hands and said, "Or we'll be in the front row. All the seats will be sold out except the front row."

It was early afternoon on a Saturday in November. The blaze of color on the mountains had gone out, but snow had yet to fall. In the Salt Lake Valley, winter had come down hard, which meant Jem had been forced to dig out his coat: heavy, undyed wool with broad bands that ran across the chest in red, yellow, blue, and green. Tean had also apparently felt the cold since he was wearing an enormous brown coat with the Division of Wildlife Resources logo on the sleeves. He was sweating.

"And our necks," Tean said, jogging again to close the gap. "You know what sitting in the front row will do to our necks?"

"Not yet."

"We'll probably do permanent damage to the cervical vertebrae."

"Uh oh."

"We won't be paralyzed—"

"Good; I was worried."

" — but we'll be in excruciating pain for the rest of our lives."

"Right."

"And probably get addicted to opioids."

"Probably."

"And end up selling our bodies on the streets to get our next fix."

"Together?"

Tean forced his glasses back up his nose. "What?"

"Are we going to sell our bodies on the streets together?"

"I don't understand what you're asking me."

"Well, you kept saying, 'we,' so I'm just trying to figure out if we're going to be working the same corner, or if we're like a combo package, you work the top and I work the bottom, or if — are you ok?"

"It's this dang coat," Tean said, wiggling out of it. His cheeks were bright red, and sweat streamed down his face. "When I wear it in the field, it's great, but I don't think it's meant for, you know . . ."

"I think I know," Jem said.

Tean wiped his face, hugging the coat to his chest with one arm.

"It's heat stroke," Jem said.

Pausing mid-wipe, Tean stared at him.

"Yep," Jem said. "Definitely heat stroke. And you're going to die from it — sorry about that — because your body is overheating and can't cool down fast enough. It's going to fry your brain."

"No, I'm sweating, so I'll be fine —"

"And then I'm going to tell them not to keep you alive artificially because you wouldn't want that —"

"I do want that, actually."

" — and I'll tell them to chop you up and donate all your organs and make the rest of you into chum for people that want to swim with sharks."

"No! I hate those people. They absolutely should not be swimming with sharks!"

"And some poor lady who's always dreamed of being a bus driver, but she can't because she's been blind her whole life, she's going to get your eyes. Only you have such bad vision that she'll drive the bus right off a cliff. And it'll be full of orphans. And boom, crash, whoosh, crackle, char-roasted orphans."

Tean stopped in the middle of the sidewalk, clutching the coat to his chest, eyes wide. "What is going on here?"

Cocking his head, Jem said, "Hey look, we made it. Hold on while I score us tickets."

"What about the orphans?" Tean shouted after him; then he caught the eye of a lady who was staring at him as she herded children down the sidewalk, and he hunched his shoulders, his face burning.

"Two," Jem said, holding up his fingers to the girl sitting inside the ticket booth. "For the 2:30 *Ragnarok,* please."

"Sorry, that showing is sold out."

"What about two seats that aren't together?"

She didn't even look down at the screen. "Nope. Sold out."

"Ok, what about the 3:15 showing?"

"Sold out."

Glancing over his shoulder, Jem saw Tean tapping frantically on his phone, probably trying to figure out the actual roasting temperature of orphans or something like that. To the girl in the booth, Jem said, "What about the front row?"

"Sir, it's sold out."

"Sir?" Jem said.

She stared at him, dead eyed, slack jawed.

"What about the 4 —"

"Sold out." Then, mustering what looked like a tremendous amount of energy and initiative, the girl added, "It's opening day, sir. They're all sold out."

"Sir?" Jem said again.

"I told you," Tean muttered, dragging him away from the ticket booth. "I told you it would be sold out. I don't know why you even want to see this one. I heard there's this movie about a child with a birth defect and it's really wonderful."

Jem looked at him until Tean's cheeks reddened again.

"If someone else said it," Tean muttered, "it would sound normal."

"I don't want to see that one. I want to see Chris Hemsworth, and I want to see him with a lot of muscles and ripped shirts, and I want to see him with the super short, hot-as-fuck new haircut, and also I want him to fly around and zap things with lightning. And since you are getting less action than a seventh-grader at a middle-school dance, I figure you'd enjoy seeing Chris Hemsworth too."

"Is he an actor?" Tean said.

"Thor, The Avengers, Thor: The Dark World, Avengers: Age of Ultron." When Tean didn't respond, Jem added, "He was even the captain at the beginning of *Star Trek.*"

"Is that the one with Yoda?"

Jem covered his face with both hands.

"I told you I hadn't seen the other ones," Tean said.

"It's not—you're missing out on—" Jem dropped his hands. "You know what? Never mind. I'm going to fix this. I'm going to get us tickets to this movie—"

"If we're in the front row, the damage to our retinas—"

"Not in the front row," Jem snapped. He took a breath and repeated, "Not in the front row. I'll get us good seats to this movie. Just hang out here; I'll be right back."

Tean caught his arm.

"They're going to start seating people in a few minutes," Jem said, trying to shake him loose. "I've got to hurry."

"No breaking any laws," Tean said. "If we're going to be friends, I don't want you breaking any laws when we hang out."

"Fine, fine. Will you get off of me?"

"And no lying."

"Come on."

"I'm serious: no lying."

"Yes, all right, whatever. Can I have my arm back?"

"I'm serious, Jem."

Jem rolled his eyes, worked Tean's fingers loose, and jogged toward the ticket booth again.

2

Waving the fifty-dollar gift card that he had just bought with cash at the ticket booth, Jem made his way up and down the line of people waiting to see *Thor: Ragnarok.*

"I'm serious," Jem announced as he repeated his offer. "Fifty bucks for two tickets to see this movie. I'll walk up to the ticket booth with you, and you can verify that the gift card has money on it, and then you pass over the tickets."

A big guy wearing a backward Jazz hat, a North Face jacket, Under Armour gym shorts, and Nike slide sandals, sneered and looked at his buddy, who was wearing an identical ensemble.

"Fifty bucks," Jem announced again.

A group of teenage girls clustered together, giggling as they glanced over at him.

Normally, Jem's routine would have been different. Based on this crowd, mid-afternoon—a lot of kids, teenagers, and families—he probably would have tried for a mixture of sympathy and moralized self-satisfaction. He'd have figured out the row of seats he wanted, picked a pair of numbers near the middle of the theater, and called them out. Then he would have explained to the unlucky couple that the theater had made a mistake: he was supposed to take an underprivileged kid—or maybe, in another version, he was helping with the Make-A-Wish Foundation—to see this movie, only the theater had canceled his tickets. He'd work the line until somebody was willing to turn over their tickets for cash, although a lot of the time, especially in Utah, people just surrendered the tickets for free.

Today, though, with Tean's stipulations (nothing illegal and no lies), Jem had to be a little more creative.

"Fifty bucks," Jem shouted. "Come on. Somebody? Anybody?" He checked behind him, glad to see that Tean was busy inspecting a pigeon, and added, "What if I tell you it's for true love?"

Jazz Hat made a gagging noise.

The teenage girls were giggling even more intensely, and then some sort of internal struggle seemed to resolve itself, and they pushed one girl forward. She was black, her braids pulled over one shoulder, and she played with her hair as she looked at Jem, and then away, and then back.

"Um, hi," she said.

"Please tell me," Jem said, "that you're going to help me out. This is crazy love. Real, deep, fairy-tale level true love."

"Um, like, my friends and I want to help you, but, um, there are five of us."

"Well, maybe two of you want to do something else. Maybe two of you want to head up to City Creek and hang out for a couple of hours."

"Is, like, your girlfriend already here?" For some reason, that made the other girls burst into giggles, pressing closer together as they whispered to each other.

Jem grinned. "Kind of, but we're not exactly together. Yet."

"Oh my gosh, she must be super pretty because you're, um, gorgeous."

More giggles. The poor girl was playing with her braids like she was about to rip them out of her head, but she also looked pleased with herself, proud of her own forwardness.

"Well," Jem said, "I'm actually more, you know, Chris Hemsworth than Natalie Portman, if you get what I mean?"

The girl's eyes got huge, and she retreated into the gaggle, the girls exploding with laughter as she rejoined them and repeated what Jem had said.

"Faggot," Jazz Hat coughed up the line. His buddy laughed.

Jem checked his pockets: paracord and hex nut, telescoping antenna, barrette, empty tube sock. He had one fist tight around the antenna as he met Jazz Hat's gaze, winked, and blew him a kiss.

Jazz Hat's face went red, and he turned redder when his buddy laughed again.

"Fifty bucks," Jem shouted. "Double your money right now. I don't care where you're sitting."

A whistle interrupted him. Near the end of the line stood a middle-aged couple, and the woman waved. Jem trotted to meet them. The man was in a shapeless khaki jacket that made him look a little bit like a peanut; Tean would have loved it. The woman was in a trucker's jacket that flared at the hips.

"We drove all the way up here from Sandy," she said.

Jem nodded.

"And I work most weekends."

Jem nodded again.

"And we're going to have to cancel our dinner reservations."

"Well," Jem said, "let's see if we can avoid that. What if you went to the mall and spent a couple of hours shopping?"

"Melvin hates shopping," the woman said, grabbing the man's arm. "Tell him, Melvin."

Melvin grinned vacantly and nodded.

"You two look like you're a sophisticated couple," Jem said, remembering too late his promise not to lie. "I could have my friend at the Apollonia's bar set you up with some cocktails and appetizers. You know, a little pre-dinner relaxation."

The woman had already gone ramrod straight, her fingers biting into Melvin's bicep. "We don't drink," she said. "And we don't go to bars." She started to turn away from Jem.

"My mistake," Jem said in a rush. "I'm sorry about that. What about this? You head up to the Clark Planetarium, and that way you can stay in the city and still go to dinner when you're ready."

The woman tugged on her trucker jacket. Her eyes didn't shift once to Melvin, who was staring at the movie posters lining the wall.

"But we're still going to miss the movie," she said, her eyes cold and calculating.

Jem extended the gift card.

"I really don't know," the woman said. "Melvin had his heart set on this movie."

Melvin was looking around like he'd been kicked in the head by a horse.

"I can tell," Jem said. "What about this? I throw in some cash so you can see one of the IMAX movies at the Planetarium. And you reserve your *Thor* tickets today, with the gift card, so you get good seats for next time." He smiled and said, "Please? This would really mean a lot to me and my friend. You're seriously my only chance — did you see how everybody else treated me? They looked right through me. You're the only one who's been decent enough to even consider helping me out."

The woman hemmed.

Jem took two twenties out of his pocket.

"Well," the woman said after she had checked the gift card and counted the cash. "That's all right then."

"You're a saint," Jem said. "Honestly, you have no idea how much this will mean to my friend. He won't even care that we can't get snacks because I gave you my cash. Will you come over here and meet him? I know he'll want to thank you too."

She blushed a little and shook her head. Then, after a slight hesitation, she passed back the cash.

"I couldn't," Jem said.

"Please," she said.

"No, no. That's yours. I want you to have a nice afternoon."

"We'll have a wonderful time at the Planetarium, and those IMAX movies give Melvin vertigo." Smiling, she pressed the money into Jem's hand. "You know, you remind me a little of my grandson."

When she held out the tickets, Jem snagged them and sprinted back to Tean; the people in line were already heading into the theater.

3

"These are in the front row," Tean said, examining the tickets.

Jem groaned.

"I'm sorry," Tean said. "It'll be fine."

"No," Jem said. "Your neck."

"I'll wear a brace."

"Your retinas."

"I'll get those really dark sunglasses that blind people wear sometimes."

Jem snatched the tickets back.

"Seriously," Tean said, "it'll be fine. I really appreciate how hard you—"

"I'm going to fix this."

"No, Jem, please—"

But Jem was already jogging toward the theater. He passed one of the tickets to the girl collecting them, accepted his stub in return, and headed into the darkened passageway. Freshly popped popcorn. The sound of rubber soles ripping free of the sticky floor. Once, Jem and Benny had gone to the six-pack theater in Tooele with nothing but twenty bucks between them—LouElla had given them the money to get them out of the house—and they'd spent a whole Saturday hopping from movie to movie and gorging on half-finished buckets of popcorn, boxes of Mike and Ikes abandoned in cupholders, and all the Mountain Dew they could drink courtesy of free refills in the cups they'd washed out in the bathroom sinks.

The electric sconces shed dim cones of light up the walls, enough for Jem to see that the seats were mostly filled. On the main level, where he stood, several decent seats were open, but they were all reserved for people with disabilities or people accompanying someone in a wheelchair. From what Jem could tell, they'd gone unsold for today's showing, the only open seats in the sold-out theater.

Jem scanned higher up the stadium seating; he had promised Tean a good spot. An older man in a trucker hat, speaking too loudly into the ear of a woman who might have been his daughter — although his hand was sliding a little too far up her thigh. Four boys who had to be eleven or twelve, chucking kernels of popcorn at each other until one of them, a thin-faced kid with a rattail, switched the game up with a quarter, and then another boy was shouting and clapping a hand to his face. A young mother, an infant against her shoulder. Only in Utah, Jem thought. A group of middle-aged women sat together, all of them wearing homemade t-shirts with Chris Hemsworth as Thor on them —

Crying pulled Jem's attention back to the young mother. She was round-faced, no makeup, in a t-shirt and sweatpants cut off at the knee, ragged threads hanging against pale, thick calves. She was with a friend, Jem realized — another mom, this one with dark hair in a severe bob, rocking a carrier between her legs. With one hand, the round-faced woman mechanically patted the baby's back; her gaze was fixed on the screen, where some sort of question was being asked — four options, A-D, were also presented. The infant squalled, its tiny legs working under the thin blanket.

The man in the Jazz hat, whom Jem had noticed in the line, was seated right behind the women. Loud enough for the whole theater to hear, he said, "This is ridiculous; I paid for this. I paid good money to see this movie."

The round-faced woman sat stiffly.

"That's the problem with this whole state," Jazz Hat was saying to his buddy, who was nodding so vehemently he looked like he'd suffered a neck injury. "Everybody just wants to pop 'em out, and then everybody else gets screwed. I paid twelve bucks for my seat, and I could have heard kids crying at home."

The round-faced woman and her friend might have been cast from iron.

"'Scuse me," Jem said, working his way down the row. "Thanks, sorry, thanks, thanks." He dropped into a squat. "Hi, sorry to bother you."

The dark-haired woman didn't even look over. The round-faced woman glanced at Jem, her hand still beating out a rhythm on the infant's back, before she looked at the screen again.

"I hope I'm not being out of line here—"

"We can bring 'em in," the round-faced woman said. "Jennifer."

The dark-haired woman, presumably Jennifer said, "There's no law or nothing that says we can't."

"Oh no," Jem said. "I'm not here to complain. Actually, I just wanted to see if I could do you a favor."

Jennifer looked at him for the first time, and then she leaned toward the round-faced woman, whispering in her ear. The round-faced woman stared straight ahead, but her face colored.

Jem decided to add a smile. "My friend and I have some seats near the front, and I was wondering if you wouldn't mind shuffling around. See those seats on the main level, the ones reserved for people with disabilities? I was wondering if you'd like to have them instead. You wouldn't have to sit by, well, certain people. And if one of the babies starts to cry, it'd be easier to take him out. You wouldn't have to crawl over everybody in the row, you know? And you could come right back in, no problem."

In the next row, Jazz Hat was glaring at Jem, obviously trying to figure out what was going on.

The round-faced woman leaned over, whispering something to Jennifer, and Jennifer whispered something back.

"Hey," Jazz Hat said. "Hey, what are you doing?"

Jem and the women ignored him.

"They're down low," Jennifer said.

"Well, they're not as high as these seats," Jem said. "That's true. But they're still pretty good seats. And like I said, convenient in a lot of other ways." He cut his eyes up to the next row as he added, "Plus, you won't have to breathe Drakkar Noir the whole movie."

Jennifer giggled.

"Why don't you come down and take a look?" Jem said. "See if you like the view."

Another whispered consultation, and then the round-faced woman nodded.

"What's going on?" Jazz Hat said. "Is there some kind of problem?"

"There is," Jem said, meeting his eyes and then looking back at the women. "We've had complaints about this section of the theater smelling like a frat boy jockstrap."

Both women burst out giggling.

"What the hell?" Jazz Hat said. "Bobby, did you hear this guy?"

"Here," Jem said to the women, "I'll take the diaper bags — yeah, I got it. Don't worry." Slinging both bags over his shoulder, he slid along the row, down the stairs, and stopped at the reserved seating.

"You gotta have a wheelchair," the round-faced woman said, eyeing the blue symbol on the floor when she joined him. "You didn't say anything about a wheelchair."

"That just means someone with a disability," Jem said. "Pregnant and new mothers, that counts too."

"Jennifer has diabetes, but she couldn't get that special parking."

"You know what?" Jem said. "I've got an idea. But first, let's see if you like the view."

The women sat, arranging diaper bags and children and snacks. That was half the battle; inertia might keep them seated even if they hated the view. But after another quiet chat, the women looked up and nodded.

"Great," Jem said. "Great. I'll check with the theater manager, just to make sure it's ok. Right now, though, I'm going to get my friend. Thanks for being so flexible."

But when he turned around, heading out of the theater, he stopped. Jazz Hat was standing in the passageway that led back to the lobby, talking to a woman in a theater-employee uniform: a maroon vest, white shirt, maroon trousers. A little bit like a bellhop. She had brushed on a couple of miles of turquoise eyeshadow to complement the getup.

"That's him," Jazz Hat said. "That's him. He's been scalping tickets and making people change seats. And I paid twelve American dollars to see this movie."

After a long, turquoise blink, the woman said to Jem, "Sir, could you come with me, please?"

4

"We're going to get banned for life," Tean whispered as he and Jem followed the theater manager toward her office. "And then it's going to go public. And I'm going to get accused of abusing my position."

"Your position as a wildlife veterinarian," Jem said.

"As a government employee. And I'm going to get dragged in front of one of those ethics review boards."

"I don't think—"

"And there will be a public scandal."

Jem sighed.

"And I'll get fired." Tean's huge, dark eyes blinked, seeming distant as he considered this future. "And I'll never be able to work again."

"What's her name tag say?"

Tean blinked again. "What?"

Jem gestured to the woman ahead of them.

"Oh. Meredith."

"Gotcha. Thanks. Also, positive spin: maybe you'll get to use those cool vet skills to do something way more awesome. Awesomer. No, more awesome sounded better."

"No," Tean said, shoving his hands in his pockets. "I won't."

"Maybe you'll move to Vegas and work for the mob. Maybe you'll be stitching guys up and doping people with ketamine and getting lightbulbs out of asses."

"What exactly do you think vets do? What do you think the mob does, for that matter?"

Jem grinned at him.

"Anyway, that's not going to happen," Tean said. "I'll probably end up as a lot lizard, sucking off truckers for a few bucks."

"And then you'll get mouth AIDS and die."

"What the heck? Jem, you cannot say stuff like that. You can't joke around like that. And there's no such thing as mouth AIDS." Tean seemed to consider something and added, "And I'll probably get run over by a tractor trailer. Squashed into a paste. There won't even be enough left of me to put in a casket."

"Plus side," Jem said, "talk about major financial savings. We can just put you in that box on the shelf in your closet."

Tean's eyes got huge. A flush worked its way under light brown skin, and his jaw dropped.

"You know," Jem said, "the one where you keep all those old Hollister calendars."

"You can't—I don't—they're historically significant—" With what looked like a great deal of effort, the doc pulled himself together. "Friends don't snoop in each other's stuff, Jem."

"I'll remember that," Jem said. "But I did notice that Mr. December 2011 has suffered a lot of wear and tear."

"Shut up."

"Torn edges, of course. And the fact that the page practically fell out of the calendar."

"No, really: shut up."

"But I was most curious about the spotting that looked like water damage—"

Jem was laughing as the doc pushed him into the wall.

"I'm going to kill you," Tean said.

"Let me get us out of this jam first, please."

The office was small, with most of the space taken up by a desk, chairs, and filing cabinets. On the walls, old movie posters offered a brief march through history: *The Patriot, Frida, Apocalypto*. The tight space smelled like rancid oil and an artificial lavender air freshener. Meredith sat behind her desk.

"Gentlemen, I'm very sorry to do this, but I'm going to have to refund your tickets and ask you to leave."

"Of course," Tean said. "That's fine. Thank you. Um, and, sorry?"

When the doc turned toward the door, Jem caught his wrist. "No," he said. "I don't think so."

"It's not up for debate," Meredith said. "We have a clear policy against re-selling tickets and trading seats—"

"Bullshit."

"—and we take patron satisfaction very seriously." Meredith's cheeks were almost the same shade of maroon as her uniform. "I'll be happy to give you your money in cash or as a gift card, but I'm afraid you won't be seeing your movie today."

Jem took a moment, trying to make the math work: how quickly Jazz Hat's complaint had reached a manager, Meredith's decision to drag them to this cubbyhole instead of confronting them in the lobby or the theater, the heightened color in Meredith's face, the rapid breathing.

His grip slid down, and he laced his fingers with Tean's. The doc immediately started squawking and trying to pull free, but Jem held on grimly.

"I guess it's because I'm sexually attracted to men," Jem said. "I guess that's what's happening here. That asshole in a Jazz Hat scurried off to tattle, and as soon as you heard that a couple of faggots were in your theater, you decided you had to get rid of us to keep all the decent, God-fearing folk from realizing what kind of disreputable establishment you run."

"That's absolutely not —" Meredith said.

"You think people don't know what's been going on here?"

"Sir, everyone is welcome —"

"You think this isn't going to hit the news? You think corporate doesn't already know about the ongoing shitshow you're running?"

"This has been a misunderstanding," Meredith said. "This has all been a huge misunderstanding."

Tean was using his other hand to try to pry Jem off him.

"Stop it," Jem snapped under his breath. To Meredith he said, "We're going to watch our movie. And we're going to enjoy some complimentary popcorn, soft drinks, nachos, pretzels —"

"Good Lord," Tean murmured.

"—and movie candy while we do."

"There's no such thing as movie candy," Tean said. "It's just candy."

"How does that sound?" Jem asked. "Otherwise, I'll call the *Deseret News* and see if they're interested in a feature piece."

Less than five minutes later, they were standing at the concessions counter, while Meredith explained to a bewildered, acne-speckled teen that they were to be given whatever they wanted.

"And extra butter," Jem shouted as the teenager scurried off to get the popcorn.

"What just happened?" Tean said.

"The butter is the best —"

"No. In there."

"Oh. I don't know. She's obviously scared about something."

"About what?"

"I have no idea."

"So that was—"

"Oh, yeah, pure bullshit."

Tean shook his head.

"It's like I told you," Jem said, "people will believe anything if they want it to be true. Or if they're afraid it is."

"Uh huh." Tean brought out his phone and tapped the screen a few times.

"What?"

"According to this, a theater patron called the police on a black family a few weeks ago," Tean said. "I guess Meredith the Manager didn't want a repeat PR disaster. Didn't want to make the Jazz Hat guy any angrier, but didn't want us to make a public scene either."

"There you go." Jem tapped the glass and called to the acne-covered kid, "No Raisinets, you hear? Don't even think about it. I want the good stuff."

When they made their way toward the theater, though, Jem swore.

"What?" Tean said, juggling the six boxes of Butterfinger Bites that Jem hadn't been able to carry.

Jazz Hat was coming out of the theater doors, and when he saw them, he stopped and folded his arms.

5

"What are you doing here?" Jazz Hat asked.

"I bought a ticket," Jem said.

"Two," Tean said.

"I bought two tickets," Jem said.

Jazz Hat stepped into their space, arms still across his chest. He was a big boy, standing taller than Jem, broader in the chest and shoulders, with a gut that suggested pretzels and—even though this was Utah—maybe a few beers after dinner. "You didn't buy those tickets," he said. "You tricked those old people into selling them to you."

"If anything, they tricked me. They wanted me to buy their damn IMAX tickets too."

"Wait," Tean said, "what?"

"You think I haven't noticed what you've been doing? You've been bothering people."

"Bothering people," Jem said. "That sounds like a felony."

"The rest of us play by the rules. We bought our tickets. We reserved our seats. We did it all in advance. Your type always thinks they get to be the exception."

"My type?"

"Blonds," Tean said.

"Hey."

"Well, he's not wrong."

"What the hell, Tean?"

"I'm just saying most blonds are kind of, um, awful."

"I cannot believe this. I cannot believe I'm on a date with an anti-hairist."

"First of all," Tean said, "this isn't a date."

"I knew it," Jazz Hat said, a finger stabbing out toward them. "I knew you two were fagging out on each other."

"And second of all, there's no such thing as an anti-hairist. I don't even know what that means."

"It means you hate people because of their hair color. I take really good care of my hair. I've got great hair."

"You ought to after all those haircuts," Tean murmured.

"Excuse me?"

"Hm?"

"What was that?"

"What was what?"

Jazz Hat seemed to realize he had lost control of the conversation because he bulled towards them again. "Listen, this shit might fly in Rhode Island, but this is a good place with good, God-fearing people, and —"

"It's a high-maintenance style, Tean. It's practically shaved on the sides and back."

"I noticed. Very skinhead chic."

"And to keep it short, I need regular — holy shit. Holy shit. Did you just call me a skinhead?"

"Watch your language," Jazz Hat said, grabbing Jem by the shirt. "There are families here?"

"Soccer player," Tean said. "I should have said soccer player chic. Futbolista chic. Is that better?"

JEM + TEAN: GUYS GONE WILD

"Than skinhead? Damn it, of course that's better. Tell him."

Jazz Hat seemed surprised by the sudden direct address, and his forehead furrowed as he stared at Jem. Then he turned to Tean and said, "Soccer player is better than skinhead."

"Noted," Tean said.

For a moment, Jazz Hat's hand worked restlessly on Jem's shirt, and he looked around the lobby. Then, his voice gaining strength, he said, "Now, I'm going to march you two faggots out of here, and you better never—"

"This is about to get ugly," Jem told Tean.

"Can't you just, you know, do that thing where you smile and say, 'Aw, shucks,' and everybody just gives you what you want?"

"I've never in my life said, 'Aw, shucks,'" Jem said, "and anyway, that doesn't work on assholes. That's why an enterprising young man like myself needs a versatile skill set."

"I really think we should—"

"Hold this," Jem said, shoving a paper cup of Mountain Dew at Jazz Hat. The bigger man reacted automatically, grabbing the cup. Jem planted his free hand on Jazz Hat's chest and pushed. At the same time, he hooked one foot behind his ankle, and the big man went down, the fluorescent-green soda drenching him.

"Frick, frick, frick," Jazz Hat said, running his hands over the North Face jacket and the Under Armour shorts. "Oh my gosh!"

"Don't escalate," Tean said.

"Never," Jem said.

"I'm serious: no violence."

"So many goddamn rules."

As Jem approached Jazz Hat, the big man tried to push himself up. Jem was faster, though, dropping one sneaker on Jazz Hat's chest and forcing him back down. Everybody else in the lobby stood frozen in place, watching the scene unfold. The popcorn machine was going like gangbusters.

"Stay," Jem said to Jazz Hat. "And listen really carefully. All I wanted was to see Chris Hemsworth with his ultra-hot short haircut and go on a nice date with my boy here."

"It's not a date," Tean announced to the lobby. He caught the eye of a blue-haired woman clutching a change purse to her chest and repeated, "It's not a date. At all."

"Jesus, Tean," Jem snapped. "It can be a friend date."

Tean sighed.

"We can have an epic fucking bromance," Jem said.

"I think the previews are starting."

"Do you see what I have to put up with?" Jem said to Jazz Hat. "Do you see how my life is a constant, uphill battle?"

"It's the haircut," Tean said. "Too much upkeep."

Jem shot him a glare. Then, to Jazz Hat, he said, "Stay the fuck away from us. Understand?"

Jazz Hat looked extremely confused and, to Jem's disappointment, more worried about his Mountain-Dew-soaked clothing, but he nodded.

"Take a few breaths and eat some candy," Tean said to Jem, handing off several boxes of Junior Mints. "I'll get you another soda."

6

The lights dimmed. The first preview came on — an action sequence, a guy running down a tunnel, thunderous music. Jem put his arm around Tean.

Tean pushed his arm off.

"I think I was really brave today," Jem whispered.

Tean nodded and tossed back some popcorn.

"And very creative."

Another nod.

"I mean, I got us these tickets, and I got us all this candy, and I didn't lie or do anything illegal. And I got rid of that jackass without using violence."

"You shoved him."

"Well, that was before I knew about the new rule."

The first preview ended, and the next one started: a creepy doll in a Victorian-style dress, her little porcelain head spinning round and round. A woman farther down the row screamed, and then laughter rippled through the theater.

Jem tried again to put his arm around Tean's shoulders.

This time, Tean caught his wrist early and pinned his arm to the seat.

"Not a date," Tean whispered.

"It's a friend date."

"Not a romantic date."

"That's ok. I'm ok with that. We talked about that. We're just friends."

"And you put your arm around all your friends when you watch movies?"

"Sure," Jem said, slinging an arm around Tean and pulling him close. "Whenever we share popcorn." He grabbed a handful of kernels from the bucket in Tean's lap to demonstrate.

Tean shook himself like a wet dog, but Jem held on.

"Do you have any Reese's Pieces?" Jem asked.

Tean didn't answer; he was too busy trying to sink down into his seat to escape Jem's touch.

With a sigh, Jem pulled his arm back. "Reese's Pieces?"

Straightening up in his seat, Tean passed him the box of candy.

The next preview was Chris Pine and a lot of glass breaking and cars exploding. And the next was an actress Jem didn't recognize; she was swimming in a lake, at night, and the frenetic music meant something terrible was about to happen.

When Jem reached for the popcorn, he bumped Tean's shoulder. The next time, it was his elbow. And the next time, he leaned right into Tean's field of view.

Hissing in frustration, Tean shoved the popcorn bucket toward Jem. "Here. You hold it."

"Oh, no way. I don't want to ruin my jeans."

Tean was growling. It was a cute, puppyish kind of growl. "Fine," he snapped.

Jem put his arm around Tean.

"This is not a date."

"See how much easier this is?"

"I want you to hear me very clearly."

"I heard you. Not a date. Got it."

Tean squirmed for a few minutes, obviously fighting an internal battle between his dislike of being touched and the desire for Jem to stop bumping him every time he got popcorn.

"Just cool down," Jem whispered, giving Tean a squeeze. "I'm not going to try anything."

"Ha."

But after another minute, Tean relaxed. And after a few more minutes, he rested his head on Jem's shoulder.

The theater darkened completely for an instant, and then the film began.

"Good thing, by the way," Jem whispered.

"What?"

"Good thing this isn't a date."

In the flickering light from the projector, Tean's face betrayed another struggle. Finally he said, "Why?"

"Because I've only got eyes for one man today, and he's the Asgardian god of thunder. With a high-maintenance haircut, which you wouldn't understand because you've got that Latino baby Einstein thing going—"

The charley horse came so hard and fast that Jem never had a chance to protect himself. Groaning, he massaged his knee.

"Holy Mother of God," he whispered. "I think you pinched a nerve."

"You know what?" Tean said, shaking out his hand. "I think I like friend dates."

Even with his leg on fire, Jem couldn't help smiling.

SUPERTROPE: THE BIRTHDAY EPISODE

This story takes place before *The Same End*.

1

Buffy was trying to catch Angel. Or maybe she was trying to catch another vampire. Her face was flushed. Strands of blond hair whipped behind her. The background was dark and hazy, with lumps that might have been tombstones. A cemetery, Tean guessed. Or maybe a public park with sinkhole issues.

"They should do a special episode," Tean said. "Those are popular, right?"

Jem was curled up on the couch next to him, head pillowed on his arm, eyes fixed on the TV. "Well, the show ended twenty years ago, so I'm not sure that's in the cards."

"They could do a special episode about how she conquered her eating disorder."

"She doesn't have an eating disorder."

"Undiagnosed, then. The shape of her face, her neck, when you can see her ribcage—"

"No!" Jem shot upright. Something had happened on the show, but Tean had missed it.

Scipio, who was sulking on his bed after not being allowed to climb on top of Jem, raised his head and woofed once. Bandages still covered Jem's arms, and no matter how much he insisted he was ok around Scipio, Tean was trying to keep the black Lab from overwhelming Jem with his love.

"It's fine," Tean said.

"It's not fine. Oh my God, he's Angelus now." Jem slumped in the other direction, his head landing in Tean's lap. "If you were paying attention at all, you'd know this is definitely not fine."

"I feel like this is a ploy to get your head in my lap."

"Be quiet and do that thing I like."

"I think the #MeToo movement has taught us that you can't—"

"Tean," Jem whined.

With a sigh, Tean carded his fingers through the dark blond hair. Jem kept it in a hard side part, always perfectly combed. For some reason Tean couldn't explain, he took an indecent amount of pleasure in mussing it, sifting the silky hair between his fingers and letting it fall back in place. It had been less than a week since they'd caught a murderer. Jem had been attacked and seriously hurt, and on top of that, he'd had to come face to face with the woman who had abandoned him more than twenty years earlier. If Jem needed someone to play with his hair, well, that was the least Tean could do for him.

"Why isn't he brooding?" Tean asked.

"Who?"

"The one with the big forehead."

"You mean Angel? Literally the hottest guy on the show, the only one who's name you need to know?"

"He's not that hot."

"Scratch my neck, please," Jem answered, flopping onto his stomach, his jaw digging into Tean's thigh. "It's not up for debate, Teanomaly. He's the hottest."

"He's sulky. Someone should tell him that sulking isn't an effective way to deal with his problems."

"Well, right now he's not brooding or sulking because he's evil. He's Angelus. That's the evil version. Pure vampire. Normally vampires don't have souls because—wait, oh my God, no, don't go in there!"

"Jem, you've already seen this episode. We've both already seen this episode. We've already seen this episode this week."

"It's a good one."

"And we've watched the one where she loses her powers, which still doesn't make any sense to me—"

"It's to test her, to prove that she's worthy of being the Slayer."

"—and we've watched the one where the librarian turns into the thing with the face—"

"A Fyarl demon."

"—and the one where her fake sister runs away to fight the woman with the bad perm—"

Moaning, Jem turned his face into Tean's legs and mumbled something like, "Please stop, you're going to make me cry."

Tean's fingers froze on the back of Jem's neck. He replayed the episodes in his head. Then he said, "Jem, why are we watching these episodes?"

More mumbling that might have been: "I like them."

"These particular episodes I mean. The ones that all take place on Buffy's birthday."

Incoherent mumbling this time.

"When is your birthday?"

Jem's whole body went still.

"Jeremiah Berger." Tean tugged on his hair.

A short burst of mumbles.

"No," Tean said. "February 22 is George Washington's birthday."

Rolling onto his side, Jem said, "It can be two people's birthday."

"Is it today?"

Jem hesitated and then shook his head.

"Well, when is it? Did I miss it?"

"It's not a big deal, and that's why I didn't say anything, and — oh my God, Tean! You're going to rip my hair out!"

"I need an answer, please."

"Saturday, Jesus. May 19th. I'm going to need to see my barber. I think I've got traumatized hair roots."

"What do you normally do on your birthday?"

"Umm, have sex with strangers for money?"

Tean covered his face.

"Kidding. I do that the night before so I wake up in a nice bed on my birthday. With cash. It's a special treat."

"Ok, what about a birthday party?"

Silence.

Tean uncovered his face.

Jem was blushing, his gaze fixed on Tean's shirt, where he was trying to smooth out the wrinkles.

"You've never had one?" Tean asked.

"Well, I mean, it's not exactly like I had people climbing over each other to throw me one. And I don't want you to make a fuss about this, I just want—"

Tean pushed Jem off the couch. Seeing his opportunity, Scipio bounded off the dog bed and ambled over to remind Jem of his boundless love and affection.

"No," Tean said as he got to his feet. "Leave him alone."

"It's ok," Jem said as Scipio licked his face. "I have the feeling this is the least of my problems."

2

Buffy was very upset about something. She was crying. She'd been crying for twenty minutes, although that had something to do with the fact that Jem kept backing up and watching the same scene over and over again, but at least he was letting Tean work. Tean imagined this was the kind of temporary relief parents experienced. It explained why people spent so much money on toys.

"First, we need a theme," Tean said from the dinette table where he'd set up an emergency party-planning workstation. "The computer says we need a theme."

Now that they had the couch to themselves, Jem and Scipio were curled up together, Jem ruffling the Lab's ears. Scipio licked his arm whenever he stopped. So much for Tean's plans to keep them separate and slowly help Jem acclimate.

Tean waved one hand at the lover boys. "What about a 90s theme?"

More crying from the television.

"Or," Tean said, "we could do a *Buffy* theme."

Scipio made an outrageously contented noise, squirming around to press himself even closer against Jem.

"Or," Tean said, "because it's a birthday, we could do, you know, classic birthday party themes. Like, 'time is relentless,' or 'staring down the throat of another forty years of meaningless work in the capitalist hegemony,' or 'celebrating the unstoppable processes of DNA oxidation and DNA methylation that will culminate in the breakdown of your biological machine.' Jem?"

"Uh huh," Jem said, his attention still glued to the screen. "That one sounds good."

Tean frowned. "It'll be hard to fit on a banner. Oh. Easy. Two banners. Check. Got the theme. We'll get DNA-themed cups and plates. We can get double-helix streamers. Do you like streamers?"

No answer. When Tean looked up, Jem was wiping his teary face on Scipio's neck, and Scipio kicked a back paw in ecstasy.

"Double streamers," Tean said as he made a note. "Although, to be fair, that's not really ethical. Approximately twenty-six percent of all landfill contents are paper products, and global sustainability issues like clearcutting, emissions of methanol, benzene, nitrogen oxide, and don't get me started on carbon dioxide—"

"I won't," Jem said.

"—methyl mercaptan, hydrogen sulfide, dimethyl sulfide, dimethyl disulfide—Jem, usually this is the part you're paying attention to."

"I'm sorry." He wiped his face on Scipio again, and Scipio took this as an invitation to paw at the air until he was on his back, generously offering Jem the opportunity to scratch his tummy. Jem did. "It's just these two episodes. They get me every time. And it's Buffy's birthday, which makes it even sadder!"

"At least tell me what kind of cake you want."

"Funfetti. With funfetti frosting."

"What is funfetti?"

"Imagine if you made something that was the perfect flavor of childhood."

Tean thought about this for a moment. "Like that foot smell at the McDonald's playpen?"

Burying his face in Scipio's fur, Jem groaned. Then he went back to watching his show.

"Budget, easy. I've still got twenty-seven dollars left this month. Venue, easy. We'll do it in Liberty Park. Guest list? Who do you want to come?"

"Tean, come on. It was funny at first. Let it go."

"I'm not being funny. Who do you want at the party?"

"I don't want—" Jem jerked upright; Buffy was fighting with a sword now. Scipio barked in protest.

"Tinajas for sure," Tean said. "And her boyfriend. Fiancé? And her kids. And that guy you hook up with sometimes, what's his name? Oh, and are you dating anyone that I should invite?"

"Nice try."

"I'll figure it out. What about music? Easy again. Polka. Everybody likes a polka. Food and drink. Double easy. The park has those water stations—"

"Those are for dogs," Jem said, wincing when the swords clashed again.

"—and I'll make some appetizers."

"Um, maybe we should order—"

"Done. That was easy. I don't know why people make such a big deal out of planning parties. Or weddings, which are essentially just big parties."

"Maybe we shouldn't have a party," Jem said. "Maybe we should just order pizza, watch some *Buffy*, and have a nice night. You can put candles in the pizza, and I'll blow them out."

"No, I want to have a party. I want you to have a party. And I want you not to spend your birthday watching some dumb old show that nobody's ever even heard of."

Very slowly and deliberately, Jem raised the remote and hit pause. Then he lifted his head and turned to look at Tean. Scipio copied the movement so that two pairs of eyes were fixing Tean with identical looks of disappointment.

"What I meant to say was," Tean took a breath, "I like *Buffy*, and I think it's really a great concept. I mean, the idea that the worst punishment you can inflict on anyone is to make him immortal and then make him spend the rest of his existence in California, dealing with high schoolers, is actually wonderful. And I do like the number of decapitations. And it's nice to see a show that promotes a vision of the afterlife filled with a multiplicity of forms of eternal horrors, and not just the tried-and-true hellfire that—wait, where are you going?"

Jem jiggled open the slider. Cool spring air rushed into the apartment as he stepped outside, Scipio following.

"We're very disappointed in you," Jem said as he slid the glass door shut.

"That door locks automatically."

Jem yanked once, but it was too late. Then he lifted his chin and said through the glass, "I knew that. I'm making a point."

"What point?"

"You wouldn't understand."

"While you're out there, could you tell me if you already own DNA-related clothing to go with the party theme? Maybe a t-shirt with a damaged cell on the front? Or maybe a cell that's been hijacked by a virus and is now churning out millions of copies of the virus until it works itself to death?"

"They don't make shirts like that."

"Well, they should."

That was when Jem turned around and pretended he couldn't hear Tean anymore.

3

City Creek Mall was busy on Friday. The mall, part of a billion-dollar redevelopment of downtown Salt Lake City, was acres and acres of pale stone and glass, all of it glowing in the late afternoon sun. A small creek ran through parts of the mall, but the sound of voices and laughter covered up the noise of running water. The day was warm, with spring already threatening to tip into summer, and Tean and Jem passed through pockets of cold air where the stores kept their doors open — bursts of air conditioning that smelled like rubber soles and citrus-scented candles and bookbinding glue.

"You're going to love this store," Tean said. "I can't believe you've never heard of it."

"I want it on record that I do not need presents. I do not want presents. Today is an ordinary day. Tomorrow will be an ordinary day. I'm going to repeat that I would prefer not to have a party."

"Too bad." Tean caught his arm and tugged him down a branch of the mall that was less populated. "I went back and forth on this a million times, but I finally decided that it's more meaningful if I pick out things that I think you'll like, right? Or do you just want me to give you cash? That's what my great-aunt used to do."

Jem blinked several times. He'd spent extra time on his hair that morning, Tean could tell, and his beard was freshly trimmed. He was wearing jean cutoffs and a t-shirt with a sexualized drink pouch like the kind Tean remembered kids packing for lunch. In letters that looked like they were made out of thin, yellow plastic straws, words said, *Stick Your Straw in Me.*

"Wait, do you actually see yourself in this relationship as some sort of great-aunt-type figure?"

"You're missing the point," Tean said.

"No, I think that's a very important point."

Sighing, Tean dragged him into the novelty boutique.

"You're taking me to a store called My Big Black Hole?" Jem muttered. "Is your subconscious hard at work? Are you sending me a subliminal message about what you want to give me for my birthday?"

"It's The Black Hole, not—not what you said. And you're the one who is offering his body up as a fetishized children's drink to be harpooned by passing strangers' plastic penises."

Jem cleared his throat.

When Tean turned around, a woman was covering a child's ears. Judging by the little girl's expression, it was too late.

"He started it," Jem said from behind Tean.

"I think we should look at this as a learning experience," Tean told the woman, whose eyes were still wide with shock. "This is the perfect opportunity to teach your daughter about the dangers of over-processed, sugary drinks."

Jem groaned.

"Particularly drinks in pouches."

"Ok," Jem said, steering him by the shoulder.

"Unless you're an astronaut," Tean said, "there's no need to risk the disproportionately high chance of mold contamination that accompanies that kind of packaging. There's also scientific evidence of fungus growth; researchers found an average of five species of fungi in pouch drinks."

Jem was forcing him between racks of clothing. "You get one more, so make it good."

"Even though the pouch does contain aluminum, the layers of plastic make it almost impossible to recycle. You're not only poisoning yourself; you're destroying the environment."

"And they're gone," Jem said. "Show's over."

"No, we're not," called a little voice.

"Come on, Tamantha," the woman said, and hurried footsteps moved toward the door. "We're not shopping in a store with perverts."

"That seems like an excessively high standard for a woman who willingly decided to go inside a store called Tean's Spacious Black Hole."

Tean only managed to get in one punch before Jem caught his wrists, but it was a good one. Jem massaged his ribs as they walked up and down the aisles. More importantly, he didn't make any jokes.

"This is the one," Tean said after they'd explored for a few minutes. "This is definitely it."

It was a leather belt. Simple. Surprisingly good quality.

"That is . . . not what I expected," Jem said.

"Try it on."

Jem did. "I like it."

"It looks good on you."

"Tean, how much is this going to cost?"

"And check out the inside," Tean said.

Jem unfastened the belt and laid it flat on the counter. Words were stamped on the reverse side of the leather; the letters were ornate, which probably made it even more difficult than usual for Jem to read it. After a moment, he shook his head.

Normally Tean would have forced him to keep trying, but his excitement got the better of him. "I used to be part of a cow named Dahlia. I loved good hay, a shady spot under an oak tree, and splashing along the bank of the creek. I hope this belt was worth brutally murdering me, skinning me, and tanning my hide."

"Jesus Christ," Jem whispered.

"And it's reversible, so you can wear it with the words on the outside."

"Uh huh."

"It's a great conversation starter. You know, you can explain how everything in our lives is built on the death of other creatures, how it's impossible to live as biological machines without being participants in mass murder, and how our own mortality means that everything is pointless because we'll eventually be broken down and recycled into other forms of carbon-based matter."

"First-date kind of stuff."

"Exactly."

"Come here."

"Why?"

"I want to hug you, that's why. I don't know what I was expecting, but this is actually the best gift I've ever gotten. Which is kind of scary, now that I think about it."

Tean backed away.

Jem pushed a rolling rack out of the way and came after him.

"The hug can wait," Tean said.

"Nope."

"Yes, definitely."

"Not a chance."

"At least until I finish giving you your presents. One hug. That's all. And I won't try to squirm away for—thirty seconds."

Jem stopped. "One hug per present. Five minutes each."

"One hug total, two minutes, and I'll watch that *Darkwing Duck* movie."

Hands on hips, Jem said, "No more presents."

"Oh, no, I've already picked them out. I found you one of those shrink-wrapped blocks of underwear you said you wanted, just like the ones I buy. Remember?"

"Yes. I also remember using a very sarcastic tone."

"And a pup tent."

"The only kind of tent I'm interested in is—"

"And one of those ten-gallon hats that you said was cool when you came to my office."

"Dear Lord." Jem had on his real smile, the one showing his crooked front teeth. "I'm sorry, I'm really sorry, but I've got to hug you right now."

Tean ran.

4

"I'm just going to take it off for a minute."

Tean nodded.

"I really like it."

Another nod.

"Only because I'm worried Scipio doesn't like it."

"That might be for the best."

Legs braced, Scipio was barking wildly at Jem. When Jem removed the felt fedora, Scipio gave a final, puzzled woof and relaxed. He came across the room, nuzzled Jem's hand, and snatched the fedora in his teeth. Then he climbed back up onto the couch, trapped the hat between, his front paws, and began to lick it.

"No," Jem said. "Stop. Don't."

Tean rescued the fedora. Reshaping it, he said, "I think we can get the slobber off."

"You know what? If it's ruined, I'll pay for it. I'm so sorry."

"No, I'm the one who should be sorry. I wish we could have found a ten-gallon hat. I know Scipio would have liked that one."

Tean didn't have an accurate word for the noise Jem made.

"Ok," Tean said, once he had salvaged the fedora. He passed the hat back to Jem, who hung it from the back of a dinette chair. "I'm going to make your cake."

"We can just buy one."

"Nope. I've already got a recipe. You said funfetti, right?"

"Yes, but you don't have to make it yourself. Costco makes a great sheet cake. We can just buy one—"

"No, I want to do this. I can't believe you've never had a birthday party, and I want this one to be absolutely perfect."

"I can help you!"

"It's bad luck to see the cake before your birthday."

"I don't think that's true."

"Well," Tean said, stroking his chin, "why risk it?"

Jem tried to force his way into the kitchen, but he eventually gave up and let Tean send him back to the living room. The open floorplan meant that a mustard-colored melamine countertop was the only thing that divided the rooms, so Tean had a perfect view of Jem dropping onto the couch. Scipio immediately stood and began to pace back and forth on the couch, stepping on Jem's legs with each pass, his tail whacking Jem in the face.

"Good boy," Jem said. "Sit. Sit. Down. Play dead."

Scipio had his front paws on the arm of the couch, watching Tean in the kitchen, his tail wagging furiously.

"My eye!" Jem shouted, covering his eye. "Jesus Christ, that thing is like a bullwhip."

"Don't be a baby."

"I'm blind!"

"You're not blind."

"I've definitely got a bad case of tail-eye."

"There's nothing wrong with your eye."

"Come look at it."

So Tean went into the living room and sat on the coffee table.

"No, you need to sit over here.

So Tean moved to the couch.

"No, over here." Jem patted his lap.

"Nice try."

"I'm not trying anything. It's for medical reasons."

In spite of Jem's yelps and moans, Tean peeled his hand away. "It's a little red. He really got you good, huh?"

In answer, Scipio spun around, whopping Tean with his tail this time and knocking his glasses off his face.

Sighing, Jem picked them up and slid them back on. "Now you know my pain," he said. "Now you know what it's like to be blind."

"You're not blind. Let me get my first-aid kit. I've got drops; we'll flush it out, and you'll be fine."

Tean got the kit, and they went into the bathroom.

"Ow, ow, ow," Jem said, sitting on the toilet, trying to pull away. Tean held him in place. "It stings."

"You realize you are a very complicated man, right?"

"It's not very complicated to not want your best friend to jab you in the eye with a dropper bottle. Especially not the same eye where you're blind and you've got a raging case of tail-eye."

Tean used a clean washcloth to catch the eye irrigation solution. He dabbed it along Jem's cheekbone a few more times. Two stormy blue eyes stared back at him.

"Better?"

"Yes, thanks. It's just tragic there's no cure for tail-eye."

"Ok, I think my part in this fiasco is over."

"I'm going to have to wear a patch."

When they got back to the kitchen, Jem froze, and Tean glanced over to see that his face was totally blank.

"What?" Tean asked.

Jem pointed. "What are you making?"

"Your cake."

"But you're chopping up a beet."

"Yes."

"And crystallized ginger . . ."

"Yes."

"And—"

"Vegemite pearls. You wouldn't believe how hard it was to find those."

Jem opened his mouth. Closed it again. When he spoke, his voice had a wild edge Tean didn't recognize. "But it comes in a box! It's funfetti. It's in a box."

"Oh my gosh, you didn't believe I was going to use that, did you? First of all, it's full of things that are bad for you. The one you wanted, it had two kinds of sugar. Two. And it had trans fats. And a lot of emulsifying chemicals. And all those dyes. Yellow 5 and Red 40 are banned in Europe. Some of those artificial dyes are made from petroleum and coal tar, so—"

"But—"

"Hold on, I'm not done. That cake mix was a sure road to nausea, bloating, and spiking blood sugar. And that's just in the short term."

Jem had picked up a plastic bag. "What is this?"

"Confetti. In the long term, you're looking at diabetes, heart disease, obesity, tooth decay, liver disfunction, infertility—"

"In case you hadn't noticed, infertility isn't exactly something I'm worried about. I am, on the other hand, worried about a bag of paper confetti being included with my cake. You do understand it's a funfetti cake. Funfetti. It doesn't have paper confetti in it."

Scipio stretched on the couch and let out a doggy yawn.

"Of course," Tean said, snatching the bag of confetti from Jem's hand.

"Oh my God."

"I knew that."

"Oh my God."

"And I wouldn't have put very much in anyway because of the toxic chemicals used in processing paper, which is why we didn't get those sperm cups you wanted me to buy."

"They weren't sperm cups, and you were the one who wanted a theme for the party—"

"And that's why I bought the vegemite pearls. For the flecks of green in the cake."

"I need to lie down," Jem said.

"That makes sense. That's a classic symptom of tail-eye."

5

"You're going to wake him up," Tean said.

"I don't care if I wake him up." Ammon Young, Tean's childhood friend, former lover, and current complication, had his hands on his hips. "He's a mooch. And a bum. And he's a bad influence."

"He's tired. He got whipped in the eye with a tail."

"Do you hear yourself? Sometimes I don't even know if you realize how you sound."

On the couch, Jem stretched. Or tried to. Scipio was sprawled on top of him, and the two of them twisted around until they were both facing the kitchen. Scipio's expression changed when he noticed Ammon; Jem's did too.

"Hi, Ammon," Jem said.

"Jem. Busy day for you, I see."

"Be nice," Tean said.

"What's that smell?"

"The cake. Ammon, I'm sorry that I forgot, but I promised Jem—"

"No. That's not fair. We agreed to try doing things as friends. We made a plan. We picked a movie. We've got tickets."

"But the cake."

"Whatever is happening in that oven, you can't save it now. Come on, the movie is in twenty minutes."

"I need to walk Scipio."

"Then let's take him really quickly so we can go."

"Jem—"

"He can go the bathroom by himself, thanks."

Tean felt his face heat.

"Go," Jem said, waving lazily as he settled back onto the couch. Scipio was twisted into a pretzel, trying to get an itch, one paw flailing and catching Jem in the stomach. "I'll get Scipio outside, and I'll take the cake out of the oven when the timer goes off. You did set a timer, didn't you?"

"I was just kind of doing it like a chef does, you know? By how it looks, by the smell."

"Dear Lord. Ok, fine, I'll figure it out."

"Can we go, please?" Ammon said.

"This is the first time you've been alone with Scipio since the attack," Tean said. "Are you sure —"

"I think I can handle him," Jem said, his gaze sliding to Scipio, who had scratched his itch and was now hanging upside down off the sofa, paws already twitching in a dream.

"But if you —"

"He's a grown man," Ammon said, catching Tean's arm and dragging him toward the door. "He can take care of himself. Or he ought to be able to."

"Bye, Ammon," Jem called. "Don't get your dick caught in the hot dog roller."

Tean and Ammon were already in the hall by then, and Ammon put a hand on the door, trying to force it open as Tean pulled it shut.

"Leave it," Tean said.

"I don't know why you put up with that guy."

They went downstairs and got into Ammon's Camry. A few cardboard boxes in the back seat told another chapter in Ammon's story over the last few weeks: his marriage foundering after he had come out to his wife and family, and the fragments of his former life that kept washing up on shore.

Ammon caught Tean's glance and shrugged. "Apparently I'm entitled to the cheap set of pots and pans. Lucy's keeping the All-Clad. Don't get that look on your face," he added with a small smile. "It's better than the alternative."

"Better than the All-Clad?" Tean asked as they backed out of the parking stall. "I doubt that."

Ammon laughed quietly as he merged into traffic. They drove around the block and parked behind the dry cleaner on the next street.

"You're a very convincing actor," Tean said as they unbuckled themselves and got out of the car. "I didn't know you could do that."

"Let's just say I'm tapping into a lot of raw material." Ammon's eyes crinkled. "And if you tell anyone else this, I'll deny it, but I practiced."

In spite of himself, Tean laughed. He let Ammon boost him over the wooden privacy fence, crossing from the dry cleaner's parking lot to the strip of grass behind his apartment building. He landed awkwardly. Ammon came next, managing to make the whole thing look smooth and effortless.

"I don't know why we're going to all this effort."

"Because he's never had a birthday party, and he's one of the best people I know, and—"

"I know, I know. I meant all the sneaking around." They came around the side of the building, where an aluminum extension ladder was propped against the wall. It was angled to reach a second-story window, where the screen had been removed and the window was open. A lacy curtain fluttered in the breeze.

"He's uncannily intuitive," Tean said. "He would have figured it out."

Ammon just grunted.

"After you," Tean said, gesturing to the ladder.

"Not a chance."

So Tean went first. When he climbed through the window at the top of the ladder, he was relieved to notice that the perpetual miasma of wet cat food and floral potpourri was absent. His neighbor Mrs. Wish had an army of cats nicknamed the Irreconcilables, and Tean was doubly relieved to see that none of them was lurking in the guest bedroom, which had so much pink silk and white lace that Tean always had the impression of being trapped inside a wedding cake.

After Ammon had made his way up the ladder, they went out to the living room. Mrs. Wish was there, her white hair up in its usual bun, and she insisted on kissing them on the cheek. Tinajas, one of Jem's few childhood friends, was there, along with her long-time boyfriend Tony and her children. One of the kids, a girl who had to be in elementary school, had cornered Senator Norris, an orange tabby, and was trying to entice him with a catnip-stuffed toy. Chaquille was there—he was a grad student at the U—and Chaquille had brought a handful of other people.

"Ready?" Mrs. Wish asked.

Tean considered the banners that said *Happy Birthday, Jem*, the *Buffy the Vampire Slayer*-themed paper cups and plates, the streamers, and the enormous funfetti sheet cake from Costco.

Ammon's hand squeezed his shoulder. "It's great; he's going to love it."

Jem nodded, and Mrs. Wish tottered out of the apartment.

They heard her coming back only a few minutes later, her querulous voice floating ahead of her. " — doesn't take a veterinary genius to crawl under a bed and wrestle an angry Siamese."

Jem's voice, some sort of mumbled protest.

"Nonsense," Mrs. Wish said. "We'll have you back in a trice, and you'll be able to save that roast mutton before it gets any crispier."

This time, Jem's voice was clearer. "It's not roast mutton, it's — never mind."

When he came through the door, everyone shouted, "Surprise!"

He had made himself an eye patch out of gauze and medical tape, and he'd scribbled a skull and crossbones on the white cotton. As always, he reacted quickly. He was only startled for an instant, long enough for his hand to dip toward the pocket of his jeans, where he was undoubtedly carrying one of his improvised weapons. Then he understood. A huge smile broke out, exposing the crooked front teeth, and he started to laugh, mixing in "Thank you," and "Oh my God," and "I cannot believe this." Tinajas's kids attacked him — literally, in the case of her youngest boy, who kept trying to prove that he could knock the wind out of Jem.

Eventually, Jem managed to work his way around the room, shaking hands, hugging, kissing Tinajas and Mrs. Wish on the cheek. Mrs. Wish blushed and let out a girlish titter.

"No," Tean said when Jem got closer. "Stop. This is not allowed."

Jem hugged him so hard that Tean heard himself squeak. It was surprisingly difficult to escape, and Tean only managed it because Jem made the mistake of picking him up and swinging him around in the hug, and he was off-balance when he went to set Tean down again. That was Tean's opportunity, and he broke free.

Ammon and Jem even managed a civil handshake.

"Why is he wearing that dumb thing?" Ammon asked as Jem followed Mrs. Wish to the table when it was time for cake. "Is he a pirate?"

"Tail-eye," Tean said with a smile.

They sang. They ate funfetti cake. Someone shouted for presents.

"I already got my presents," Jem said. "Tean and I went and did that today."

"Those were, um, kind of a joke."

Jem's expression dissolved in surprise. "You son of a bitch! Ow!"

Tinajas was shaking out her hand from the punch. "Watch your fucking mouth. There are little children here, you deviant motherfucker. Now open your goddamn presents."

"Your real ones," Tean said. "Sorry about earlier. It was kind of fun to watch you squirm, though."

A Tamagotchi, an Easy-Bake oven, a Gameboy with an original Ocarina of Time cartridge, a Furby, and two unopened booster packs of Magic: The Gathering cards. Jem didn't stop laughing, didn't stop turning everything over, inspecting it, passing it around, and then inspecting it once more. His eyes came back to Tean again and again, and Tean couldn't read what he saw there.

When the party was over, everyone left. Ammon said goodnight and went upstairs. Tean and Jem were alone in the hall outside Tean's apartment.

Jem put out his arms.

"No. You already got one."

"One more," Jem said, and then he hugged Tean again.

It was very different from the first hug. Tight, but not painfully so. And vulnerable in a way that Tean hadn't known hugs could be. He was surprised to find himself hugging Jem back, pulling him tight. He was even more surprised when he felt Jem shake, and tears, hot, trickling onto his neck.

"Ok," Jem said finally, pushing free and wiping his face. "So, thanks."

"You're welcome."

Neither of them moved.

"I guess I should go," Jem said.

Go where, Tean wanted to ask. He could picture wherever Jem had ended up: another abandoned building, another vacant apartment, Jem running an extension cord so he could steal enough electricity for a lamp or a fan.

"Do you want to come in for a while? Scipio will be sad if you don't say goodnight."

"Well, I don't want to disappoint Scipio."

As they were stepping into the apartment, Tean said, "You know, surprise birthday parties are deeply problematic."

"I did not know that."

"A few years ago, a man came home and got surprised. He shot one of the guests in the head. He died instantly."

"That's why you and Ammon were standing at the back of the room today."

"And the *New England Journal of Medicine* published a study on being scared to death, which happens at more surprise parties than you'd expect."

"The old ticker just gives out."

"Exactly," Tean said. "Stress cardiomyopathy. And that's the interesting part because for a long time, people assumed being scared to death was actually a form of heart attack. It's nice to know that it's really because of a surge of stress hormones that stun the heart and cause it to stop beating."

"You know what?" Jem said, flopping down onto the couch next to Scipio. The poor Lab, exhausted from guarding the apartment all day, barely had the energy to move his head into Jem's lap. "It really is nice to know that."

"Happy birthday, Jem. Or as happy as it can be, knowing that you're inching closer to the inevitable end that awaits us all."

"Turns out," Jem said, smiling as he ruffled Scipio's ears, "that's still pretty happy."

JEM + TEAN: GUYS GONE WILD

This story takes place after *The Same End*.

1

"I said it in a moment of weakness."

Teancum Leon, wildlife veterinarian for Utah's Division of Wildlife Resources, generally considered himself a patient man. He nodded. "But you still said it."

Jeremiah Berger, con man and newly minted boyfriend, scrambled upright on the couch in their Central City apartment. It was Friday afternoon, and Tean had caught him napping. "But it was just one of those things people say."

Tean nodded again. Scipio, his black Lab, copied Jem's movement and scrambled up onto the couch. "But," Tean said, pausing to ruffle Scipio's ears, "you still said it."

Jem groaned and collapsed. When Scipio leaned over him and began licking his face, he gently shoved the Lab's head away and groaned again. More loudly.

In their bedroom, Tean set a carry-on on the bed. To get to the dresser, he had to pick a path through Jem's belongings, which now covered the floor. Convincing Jem to move in while they waited to buy a house together had been a balancing act, one that had required Tean to make certain ethical and intellectual compromises, like pretending he didn't wonder where Jem had been living, pretending not to consider the black Hefty bags full of clothes and the plastic storage bins full of shoes, pretending not to notice that some of the bags still smelled like smoke and most of them smelled like weed. At least Jem wasn't messy; everything had its own pile, its own bundle, which was probably a consequence of having never had a stable home. Frankly, Tean was surprised by how much stuff there was, although he guessed that Tinajas and Chaquille and other friends had stored some of it for Jem while he squatted in various buildings around the city.

Tean also pretended not to notice when he bumped one of the Hefties and it fell onto its side, spilling several joints onto the floor. The whole process, Tean decided, was like being invaded by a marijuana-loving, underwear-stealing, refrigerator-emptying, dog-seducing horde, and having to pretend the whole time that civilization wasn't burning down around you.

As Tean opened his drawers, he sighed again. He looked up. Jem was in the doorway, hands behind his head, his very nice arms on display. He had a body that looked hard from work rather than the gym, although Tean wasn't sure when Jem had ever done a day's work.

"I have no underwear," Tean said. "Again."

"Oh, I threw yours out."

"It was new. You just gave it to me."

"I didn't like it on you as much as I thought I would. I got you some new stuff; it's already washed, and it's, um, in that pile over there."

"Not in my underwear drawer."

"Why put it away? You're just going to wear it."

Tean sighed and opened the next drawer. He pulled out several long-sleeved tees, also provided by Jem. Some were blue, some were green, one was a color that Jem called oatmeal. That one was Tean's favorite. Some were printed with state and national park branding. Others had patterns. The whole selection was ridiculous and flamboyant and attention seeking.

"I'll be good," Jem said. "I won't tell anymore lies, and I'll make Scipio wear his harness, and I won't steal, and I won't push little old ladies in front of buses, and I'll eat one vegetable a week. Half a vegetable."

"You'd better start packing or it's going to be an uncomfortable weekend."

"I'll be so good you won't even have to tell me not to open those birthday cards that sometimes have checks in them."

"First of all, not committing mail fraud isn't an exceptionally high benchmark for being good. It's just normal, standard, decent-human-being stuff." Tean picked a path through the mounds of Jem's possessions to the pile that Jem had indicated. He gathered several briefs, held them up, and when Jem gave an absent-minded nod of confirmation, Tean said, "Are you kidding? They're practically string bikinis. I can't wear these."

Jem blinked several times. "They're low-rise briefs."

"I might as well be naked."

"Honestly, that's a great look on you too."

"I'm not —"

"I can't do this with you. I could spend a week telling you how hot you are, and how cute your little ass is, and why I'm risking death-by-boner just putting you in low-rise briefs. But I don't have time. We have a situation here. And I don't understand why you don't understand: it was just one of those things people say, Tean. It's like telling someone you'll visit them in the hospital, or when a little kid is lost in the mall and you tell them you'll help them find their parents, or when you offer to donate a kidney. They're just words. Nobody expects you to follow through on them."

"Too bad," Tean said, grimacing as he dropped the scraps of fabric that Jem called underwear into the carry-on. "We're going camping."

2

The cabin was set on Timpanogos, and dusk swooped in on the last stretch of the drive. It was November, the days mild, the nights frigid. After a quick stop at the Albertson's so Jem could pick up a few essentials, the drive had been uneventful. The aspens were still yellow and singing to each other as the mountain breeze ruffled their leaves. They passed signs for Sundance, and Jem wanted to make a joke about Better-than-Robert-Redford cake, but instead he slumped against the window and barely noticed Scipio's tongue in his ear.

They had left the main road and were following a gravel drive up increasingly narrow switchbacks, the truck bouncing over ruts, when Tean said, "I think you're too old to sulk."

"I'm not sulking. I'm pouting."

"Ok."

"Since you asked—"

"I didn't."

"—I don't like this because it's scary. Not because I don't, you know, like trees. And deer. And flowers, I guess."

"Did you bring your workbooks?"

"No."

"Did you bring your pillow?"

"Yes, obviously."

"Did you bring a backup comb?"

"I'm not going to dignify that with an answer."

"Did you bring your VHS player and your Michael J. Scott fetish videos?"

"First of all, I know you're being a jerk on purpose because you're trying to get a rise out of me. Second of all, I know you know that I brought my VHS player because you watched me pack it. And third of all, he's a fucking buttoned-down Young Republican with great hair and he looks like sex in a suit. Forgive me for knowing what I like." In a quieter voice, he added, "Especially since you're the one who benefits from it."

"What was that?"

"Don't start with me."

They doglegged around a stand of pines, and the cabin came into view: board-and-batten siding, a sharply pitched shake roof, narrow windows with glass so wavy that they might as well have been in a funhouse. The porch looked freshly swept, free of the brown needles that covered the ground, and two rocking chairs were waiting for them. When Tean stopped the truck and Jem opened the door, fresh mountain air rolled into the cab: the smell of the pines, yes, but also the crisp cleanness of the altitude and a hint of the snowcaps.

Before Jem could get out of the cab, Tean said, "I know you like to be in places you can control. I understand, a little bit, why. But you like to make me try new things, and I think you should try some new things too. You could really like this if you give it a chance."

"Oh my God," Jem said. "Now I can't even sulk without feeling like an asshole. Why do you have to make my life so difficult?"

He slid out of the car, and Scipio bounded after him. Through the closed door, he heard Tean say, "I thought you were pouting, not sulking."

"Do not start with me," Jem said over his shoulder as he approached the cabin.

The interior of the cabin was pleasant and simple, in keeping with the exterior: pine planking covered the walls and floor, and pine furniture in rustic designs filled the small living and dining area and the single bedroom. Instead of a ceiling, the cabin had exposed beams and rafters overhead. Scipio pushed past Jem, obviously interested in sniffing every square inch of space.

Jem was still looking for the thermostat when Tean came in carrying their bags. "I thought you said this place was heated."

"It is," Tean said, pointing at the stone hearth and fireplace.

"No."

"What?"

Jem put his hands over his face. "I can't. Please, God, take me in the Rapture now so I can rest in your McDonald's-special-sauce-scented bosom for eternity."

"That's a very specific eschatology," Tean said, shuffling sideways past Jem toward the bedroom. "It might be unique."

After depositing their suitcases on the bed, Tean caught Jem's sleeve and tugged him outside. They left Scipio indoors for the moment and inspected the outside of the cabin. A deck projected off the back, hanging out over ground that dropped away sharply. Ricked wood lined one cabin wall, next to a plastic storage trunk and an old, wide stump.

Tean opened the storage trunk. "I thought they said—yep. Ok, here you go."

Jem accepted the axe automatically. Then he stared at it. "What in your ever-loving mind are you thinking?"

"You can see they've already split the wood into billets—"

"I can, can I?"

"But we'll need a few thinner pieces to get the fire started. Oh, and you could shave some kindling if you wanted. That would make things easier."

"Right. Check. Shave my balls. Then shave some kindling. Got it."

Tean looked at him, and something changed in the doc's thin face. "I'm sorry. I'll do it."

"No, no, no."

"I shouldn't have—"

"Stop, I'm just being a prick. I'll do it. Do I just—" Jem brought the axe up and down. "Like that?"

"Pretty much. Let me show you how to hold it." Tean shrugged out of the quilted jacket. He was wearing a soft green flannel shirt today, and it fit the wiry lines of his body perfectly. After taking the axe, he set one of the pieces of wood on the stump—vertically, Jem noticed, which was good to know—and then he spent a couple minutes talking about the best way to hold an axe, how one hand moved with the swing. Then he demonstrated, and the blade of the axe cleaved the wood in a smooth, clean stroke.

When Tean looked over, his bushy eyebrows went up. "What? Do you want me to show you again?"

Jem swallowed. "Yes."

So Tean did it again. And again.

On the fourth time, he frowned. "You're laughing at me."

"No, I'm definitely not laughing at you."

"Go do something productive; I don't need to be your entertainment."

Jem took a step closer, eased Tean's fingers from the axe, and leaned it against the stump. Then he worked on the button of Tean's waistband and bent in to kiss him. "That was about the hottest thing I've ever seen in my entire life."

Tean chuckled, pulling back from the next kiss. "Wait. Really?"

"God, I'm going to buy you a cabin and make you chop wood all day. Fuck Alex Keaton and fuck his Young Republican haircut and fuck his suit." Jem unzipped the fly. "I'm going to show you exactly how hot that—holy Jesus Christ, fuck, fuck, fuck."

By the time he'd finished screaming, he had dragged Tean toward the tree line and away from the cabin.

"What—"

"Snake!"

The fucker had to have been almost three feet long, and it uncoiled lazily from where it had been hiding near the firewood.

"Chop it," Jem said.

"I don't have—"

"Chop it!"

"Ok," Tean said; the touch of his hand jolted through Jem. He squeezed Jem's fingers. "It's not—"

"It's got a yellow stripe. That means it's poisonous, right?"

Tean adjusted the glasses — his new glasses, which fit just right — and squinted. "I don't think it's poisonous. I think it's a gartersnake. I'm surprised it's not hibernating yet, but it might be hoping to catch one last meal."

"It almost did: us."

"No, it's—"

"If you tell me that thing is more scared of me than I am of it, I'm going to lose my fucking mind."

"Uh huh." Tean pushed back his hair with both hands. "Why don't I help him move along, then?"

Before Jem could answer this example of total verbal stupidity, Tean was already moving, kicking at the needles and talking loudly. The gartersnake slithered in the opposite direction, following the slope of the ground away from the cabin. Tean kept making noise until it was out of sight. When he came back up the hill, he grabbed the axe from where it was leaning against the stump.

"Maybe I should finish the billets," Tean said. "And you can take in the rest of the stuff from the truck. And check on Scipio so he doesn't get lonely."

"Life is so fucking unfair." Jem said, hands on his hips. "I don't even get to watch you be a lumberjack."

3

Tean fiddled with the propane tank for the stove, trying to figure out why it wouldn't work, while Jem did something on his phone that involved a lot of zapping noises and something that might have been a laser. Or a laser gun. Tean was starting to think he'd made a huge mistake.

Tean loved camping. Scipio loved camping. And this wasn't even really camping. It was camping lite. It was staying in a cabin with a fireplace and propane stove (well, in theory, anyway) and walls and a bed and running water. And Jem hated it. More than hated it. Jem probably would have rather crawled into the maw of hell, provided hell had sidewalks.

"Can I do something?" Jem asked. The sound of lasers (laser guns?) had ended. Footsteps moved across the cabin, and Scipio's claws clicked on bare boards. "You haven't stopped for five seconds.

I thought this was a vacation. I thought we were supposed to be relaxing."

Sitting back on his heels, Tean fought the urge to push his hair back. He lost. Then he said, "It's just this stove. I don't know why I can't get it to work."

"What can I do?"

"Nothing." He tried to stop there; more spilled out. "I wanted this to be fun, and I wanted you to have a good time, and I'm realizing now that this was colossally stupid."

Jem moved into his field of vision and leaned against the kitchen counter. He was quiet for a moment. Then his hand came up as he checked his hair, dirty blond and still in its hard side part. The overhead lights picked out gold in his beard. "Ok, I've been a total blowhole about this."

"No, you haven't. I should have—"

"No, I have. Attitude adjustment starts right now. Give me my marching orders, Mr.—what do you call a Boy Scout leader?"

"A Scout leader."

"Give me my marching orders, Mr. Scout Leader."

"I don't remember Scouts doing a lot of marching."

"Tean."

"Fine, fine. How about the fire?"

"Um, yeah. Sure. Do I just—"

Tean was already bending back over the tank, starting over from the beginning. "Matches are in one of the bins we brought."

"Right. Sure. Start a fire." Jem's voice firmed up. "I can do this."

But fifteen minutes later, swearing stirred Tean from his examination of the stove and accompanying tank.

"Son of a monkey's bitchfaced . . ."

Tean got to his feet, his knees protesting, and moved over to the hearth. Jem had climbed halfway inside the fireplace, contorting so he could stare up the chimney. Scipio was watching him with unwavering attention. Judging by the strand of drool hanging from the Lab's chops, Tean figured Scipio was expecting Jem to suddenly and miraculously produce some kind of snack.

When Tean tapped Jem's thigh, Jem startled, his head cracking against the inside of the chimney.

"Jesus Christ!"

"Sorry."

Emerging from the fireplace, Jem massaged his scalp. Ash was feathered across the bridge of his nose. He gestured at the pile of wood in the fireplace; next to the billets lay a stack of blackened matches.

"Something's wrong with the chimney."

Tean fought a smile. He gave Jem his hand and helped him out of the fireplace. "I think I did this all wrong."

"No, I'm going to have a great time. I've just got to fix this chimney. Do you have a broom? That's what they use on *Mary Poppins*."

"I think it's called a sweep, and that's not exactly what I meant. I love this stuff, and I just kind of hoped you'd love it too. But I shouldn't have done that. And I shouldn't have assumed you'd know what it would be like, or how to do the things I like to do."

"Well." Jem pursed his lips. Then he smiled. "Maybe you should tell me why you like it. And maybe you could help me start this fire."

Tean nodded. He got onto his knees and began rearranging the billets. "One of the things I like about camping is that it's very empowering to be able to take care of my basic needs independently. I love being out in nature, and I love the peace and quiet, but I really love knowing how to survive. Doing it like this, camping, it's like a very low-stakes test."

"Is it weird that I completely understand that?"

A smile tugged at Tean's mouth as he shook his head. "When I build a fire, I like to think of it as a lean-to. You have a big piece running in one direction, like this, and smaller pieces leaning against it perpendicularly. Then you put the kindling, if you have any, under here."

"I can do that. Now that I see it, I can do it the next time on my own."

"Of course you can." Tean passed him a match and the box with the striker strip. "Want to do the honors?"

Jem bit his lip as he dragged the match along the striker. The tip flared; the smell of sulfur dioxide floated up on a micro-thermal. He set the flame to the kindling, and after a heartbeat, the fire caught. It spread quickly, climbing up the slivers of wood until it licked along the larger billets.

Jem's grin exploded as he shook out the match. "I'm basically one of those guys from *Naked and Afraid*."

Tean wiped the soot from Jem's nose and kissed him.

"Fuck afraid," Jem said after the kiss — a little breathily, Tean was pleased to note. "I'm more interested in the naked part."

4

Sometimes, Jem thought, it was like a train wreck, and he couldn't look away.

With the fire burning steadily now, Tean had returned his attention to the stove and the propane tank. An array of tools was spread out beside him, and he picked up first one, then another, saying very un-doctorlike words under his breath.

"At this rate," Jem said, "we'll be able to afford to go to Disney World next week."

Tean's new glasses didn't slide down his face like the old ones, and with unscratched lenses, they transmitted the glare perfectly clearly.

"We'll have enough money in the swear jar to rent one of those Disney mansions, the kind with the regular sex dungeon and then a second, secret sex dungeon, and we'll have enough left over to hire some of those Disney-themed sex slaves. Yet another reason our trip to Disney World is going to be epic."

"That's not real," Tean snapped, but with enough doubt creeping in at the end to make Jem smother a smile.

"Disney World is very real," Jem said. "Trust me."

Tean grabbed a screwdriver and attacked something on the back of the stove.

"Maybe I should do that," Jem said. "I fixed your hair dryer after all."

Tean laughed so hard that he ended up on the floor, one arm across his eyes. When he'd recovered, he said, "Thank you. I needed that."

"It only burned up part of your bathroom wall. Cosmetic damage. And it worked fine the next time."

"Since I'd prefer not to be blown up, even with only cosmetic damage, I'll do it myself."

Jem decided to let that go because he'd been such an assclown about camping. "So, what's for dinner?"

Scipio, who had been feigning sleep on the couch next to Jem, perked up at the word. Laughing, Jem stroked his ears, got up, and retrieved the bowl and container of food they'd brought with them. He set them out for the Lab, who immediately began crunching kibble. He pressed hard against Jem's leg even while he ate.

Tean's answer was more swearing.

Jem opened the cooler. The Albertson's bag, full of his purchases, was buried under ice in one corner. The rest of the cooler contained what Tean had packed for their weekend.

"A container of brown gloop," Jem announced each item as he pulled it out. "Baby bella mushrooms, sliced. Eggs. Eighteen. Jesus, how many are you going to make me eat this weekend? I think this is a block of cheese, but it's now a self-contained ecosystem, so I'm going to throw it away. A bag of wet dog food."

"It's not gloop," Tean said from behind the stove. "It's that instant gravy. I already mixed it up."

"Uh huh." Jem began going through the paper sacks that held the unrefrigerated items. "Wheaties, very interesting, I honestly did not think they still made those. English muffins. Ok, I like where your head's at."

"And it's not dog food. It's a hog jowl."

Jem dropped the bag on the counter. "Why do you have a pig's face in your cooler?"

"Well, I had bought it a long time ago to make beans, but then I never used it, and then I thought you liked Egg McMuffins so much we could try to make them ourselves."

"Egg McMuffins do not have pig face on them."

"Jowl. And most foodies agree it's even better than ham."

"No. We're not doing that."

"Well, not tonight. For dinner, I'm making hamburgers."

"Ok, I'll play along. Since I didn't see any ground beef, and since I didn't see any buns, and since I didn't see any milk for the Wheaties, I'm guessing you're going to make hamburgers out of Wheaties."

"What? No. That's ridiculous. And besides, you can just put water on your Wheaties."

Jem kicked Tean's ankle. "Just tell me."

"Portabella mushrooms—"

"Oh God."

"People use them all the time as substitutes for meat."

"You don't have big portabella mushrooms in there. You have tiny, sliced-up baby bellas."

"That's why I brought the eggs. As a binder."

Scipio made a disgruntled noise and looked up, licking his chops.

"Exactly," Jem told him. To Tean, he said, "No fucking way."

"I think I can—"

"No."

Jem went out to the truck, dug through the gear, and came back inside carrying a camping grill. He used the poker to adjust the logs in the fireplace, and then he slid the camping grill over the flames. While the metal heated, he went back to the stove. Tean was lying on his back now, doing something with a crescent wrench. Jem grabbed him by the ankles, gave a warning tug, and then hauled him away from the stove.

"Jem, no!"

"Wrench."

With a sigh, Tean handed it over. Then he must have noticed the grill because he said, "What are you doing?"

"Making dinner. This is part of your continuing education course on real food humans want to eat. Wash up and then come watch me."

By the time Tean returned, Jem had unpacked some of his purchases from Albertson's. He'd anticipated a situation like this. In a bowl, he mixed ground beef, garlic powder, salt, and pepper. Then he made balls of the mixture.

"Buns are in there," Jem said. "Butter them, please."

Tean pulled a chair to the table and set to work.

"I like to start them like this," Jem said, showing Tean the balls. "Instead of patties."

"Why?"

"Because I think you get crispier edges."

Tean made a face.

Jem laughed. "What?"

"I mean, it's a hamburger. A hamburger is a hamburger."

"Uh huh. Kind of like how one snake is like every other snake: poisonous and sneaky and mean."

Tean's bushy eyebrows drew together as he considered this.

"I think it's better if you oil the pan, by the way," Jem said as he carried the plate of uncooked hamburgers to the hearth. He used a paper towel to wipe oil across the grill. "Just to help them get extra crispy."

"I'm not trying to dig in my heels, but why does it matter if it's crispy?"

"Not all hamburgers have to be crispy. But these do. Crunch is one of the things that makes food good. Salt, acid, and fat are others."

"Why do you know how to do this?"

"Because I fall asleep watching Netflix shows about food and it gets stuck in my brain." Jem set the balls of meat on the grill, washed his hands, and then used a spatula to flatten them as thin as he could. "Plus, I had to cook for myself sometimes, and I'd rather have it be stuff I wanted to eat."

"No, I mean, all of this. With the camping grill. You didn't know how to start a fire, but you sure felt comfortable doing this."

"First of all, I do know how to start a fire. I just use a lot of lighter fluid. Or gasoline. And," Jem leaned forward, patting the burgers with the spatula, "sometimes I had to cook like this. You get five seconds to feel sorry for me, and the next time I look at you, you need to pretend to be normal again." But when Jem glanced over, Tean had tears in his eyes. "Come on, Tean. I mean, I'm not happy about everything that happened in my life, but I'm fine, and honestly, I've been really lucky in a lot of ways."

Blinking rapidly, Tean cleared his throat. His voice was still froggy when he said, "I just didn't think that you might not like camping because, you know, you had to do it for real."

"I like camping with you," Jem said, "because I love you. And because we can go back to the apartment after a couple of days. And because even though all snakes are evil, especially *Mountainicus sneakicus*, which almost injected me full of poison today, I trust you to chop them if they get too close.

"Not a real snake," Tean murmured, "and snakes have venom, not poison, and gartersnakes aren't—"

"Thank God Scipio volunteered to be my second line of defense because now I know that the Big Snake industry has gotten to you. Ok, grab a plate, these are ready."

The Lab glanced over at the sound of his name, tail thumping, before returning a wistful stare to the cooking burgers.

After they toasted the buns, they carried their food to the table. Jem was watching Tean's face when he took his first bite. The doc's eyes practically glowed.

"A hamburger is a hamburger," Jem muttered, and then he smiled and bit into his own burger.

5

"I know you brought some of the cider you like," Jem said when they'd cleaned up dinner, "but are you willing to go out on a limb and trust me again?"

"That's worrisome."

"You liked the burgers. You liked the toasted buns. You agreed that crispy burger edges are delicious."

"I didn't say—"

"I know, you didn't need to. Trust me on this. I want you to try something else I like. Sit down, relax, don't look at the stove like it's your mortal enemy."

Tean dropped down on the rag rug in front of the hearth, and Scipio settled next to him, his head in Tean's lap. Jem pulled out more of his purchases from Albertson's.

"What are you making?" Tean asked.

Jem threw a quick look over his shoulder. He wanted a picture of Tean like this: all the tension unraveling, his thin shoulders relaxed, one fine-boned hand moving softly over Scipio's ears. Those bushy eyebrows were drawn together in Tean's familiar, earnest curiosity. His hair was wilder than ever after his bout with the stove.

"Hot chocolate."

Tean immediately began squirming.

"You don't like hot chocolate."

"It's fine." Tean managed almost two minutes of silence, which Jem used to mix milk and sugar and cocoa in a pot that he carried over to the grill. Then Tean burst out with: "But the cocoa trade has incredibly negative effects on the environment and on people. Most commercial cocoa farms use a lot of fertilizers that wreak havoc on local ecosystems, and labor shortages mean that people are literally enslaved to work on cocoa farms. Children do a lot of the labor, actually. Millions of kids. So that we can have waxy Milky Way bars and Hershey's Kisses."

"Fortunately, I bought fair-trade cocoa."

Tean huffed a few times before saying, "And that's not even considering the obesity epidemic in the United States and how the chocolate industry has used nutrifluff nonsense about flavanols to convince people to eat more and more high-calorie foods that have very little nutritional value."

"Definitely, definitely." Jem stirred the milk, sugar, and cocoa mixture. "Here's the good part: I can honestly and forthrightly tell you that there is absolutely nothing nutritional about this hot chocolate, and so you are not being tricked or lied to or deceived in any way."

"It's still got a ton of calories and—"

"And you're skin and bones, so we're going to consider it a dietary supplement because I'm tired of watching you subsist for weeks at a time on a single flake of oatmeal that has been bleached, crushed with a mortar and pestle, and sprinkled on a grain of wild rice. Besides, I want to get you drunk and have my way with you."

Tean blushed and ducked his chin. Jem was sitting only a few inches away on the hearth, and he cupped the back of Tean's head and pulled him in for a kiss. Then he drew Tean's head against his thigh. After a moment, Tean let out a contented breath and relaxed into him.

"I make everything so hard," Tean mumbled. "And you make it easy."

Jem ran his fingers through the unruly dark hair. "You're just a very good person, and I'm a moderately bad one."

One hand holding Jem's calf, Tean shook his head. Then he kissed Jem's knee through the denim. "You're an amazingly good person. You make my life so much better. Just you, all by yourself, you make it infinitely better, and then you find all these ways to bring other things into my life, things I can't believe I've missed out on."

"That goes both ways," Jem said, scrubbing his fingers through Tean's hair a final time. "And I've got plenty more good things I want to share with you. I brought a lot of cozy blankets, for example. I'm going to pour a fuckton of Kahlua in here, and then we're going to get wasted on hot chocolate and watch the stars before I assault your honor."

Tean smiled and kissed Jem's knee again. "I think I read a sonnet like that once."

6

The boozy hot chocolate hit harder than Tean had expected. The stars got a little blurry overhead, but he didn't mind. He was bundled up in blankets with Jem, one of Jem's arms around his waist. They built a fire in the pit on the deck, and it burned itself down to coals. The wind in the aspens. The warmth of Jem's breath. The smell of woodsmoke. The taste of Kahlua and chocolate. A million out-of-focus stars looking down on it all.

Jem's hand slid between Tean's legs, and his other hand turned Tean's face to kiss him. The kissing was good. The kissing was great. The hint of cocoa and alcohol mixing with the taste of Jem. The alternating pressure and friction that Jem applied. In spite of the stingingly cold air, Tean felt flushed. When he started to really get into it, Jem made a game out of the whole thing, pulling his hand away, chuckling as he rained kisses down on Tean's mouth and cheeks and neck.

"Jerk," Tean whispered. Then, later, with something like a whine, "Jem!"

He tried to turn the tables, tried to get a hold of Jem, but Jem was surprisingly good at finding Tean's hands and gently wrapping them in one of his own, turning away Tean's touch. It started to be too much, every inch of Tean on fire, sweat beading at his hairline, the need for Jem to touch him everywhere, touch him more, take him over this hurdle.

And, of course, Jem somehow knew that. He was the one who unwrapped the blankets and led Tean inside by the hand.

Scipio had crashed on his doggie bed, and he was snoring gently. The cabin was still warm, and the smell of pine and a fire on the hearth was pleasant. Jem undressed Tean slowly, kissing his collarbone when the skin there pimpled with goosebumps, running two fingers through the stripe of hair on Tean's narrow chest. His lips closed around one nipple, then the other, and Tean made a noise that made him blush with embarrassment. He made it again when Jem undid the tech pants and took Tean in his mouth.

Tean hovered at the edge, his hands wrecking Jem's perfect hair, while Jem was slow and patient.

When Jem stood, his hand rested on Tean's chest, guiding him back onto the bed. Then he undressed. The movements weren't intended to be provocative; Jem wasn't above striptease, as Tean had learned, but this was much, much more erotic because it was so intimate. Tean suddenly realized that Jem was nervous. It wasn't anything immediately visible like shaking hands or his posture, but Tean knew this man, could read the faint hints of hesitation.

Then Jem stood there, naked, the powerful muscles of chest and shoulders, arms and legs exposed. His body hair looked silver in the weak light that filtered through the windows, and that same light left shadows in the ripple of abdominal muscles, the crook of an elbow, the hollow of his clavicle.

He climbed onto the bed, kneeling wide, and swatted Tean's thigh. Then he swallowed.

It took Tean a moment. "Jem—"

"I want to. If you want to."

"Of course. I mean, it was great last time, but I'm perfectly happy with you . . ." The rest of Tean's sentence died away. Starlight raked Jem's beard and mussed hair, just enough light to betray the tightness around his mouth.

"I want to. With you. I want to have this with you."

Tean sat up, making space for Jem to stretch out on the bed. They kissed again. Tean kissed his lips, his nose, his jaw, his cheek. Then, clutching Tean's hair, Jem pulled Tean closer and whispered, "Quit stalling." His beard tickled Tean's neck like the start of a fire.

Tean found the bottle of lube and knelt between Jem's legs. He used one finger, not pressing, just moving in slow, steady circles. He kissed Jem's chest and belly, tasting salt and skin. When he felt a reflexive flutter, he slid his finger in, and Jem gasped.

Tean froze. "Did I hurt you?"

Jem's eyes were huge, his mouth hanging open a fraction. He shook his head.

After a moment, Tean curled his finger.

"Jesus God," Jem shouted, gathering fistfuls of the sheet. "Holy fucking Christ."

Scipio's collar jangled as the Lab raised his head and gave them a dirty look.

Tean searched again. When Jem's back bowed, and the blond man made throaty, choking noises, Tean figured he'd found the right spot.

"Do that again," Jem panted. "Fucking hell, how do you know how to make it so good?"

Tean worked carefully, slowly, relishing Jem's gasps, the way his muscles flexed and extended, how his whole body drew taut like a string being plucked. Two fingers made Jem jerk his hips in abortive thrusts.

"Fuck me," Jem said.

"I don't want to hurt you."

"You miserable teasing fuck, stick your dick in me right now."

"I want this to be perfect for you."

Jem managed to get up on one elbow. He looked like he did sometimes during their best sex, when he tipped over into a kind of fuck frenzy. Now, though, the manic desire had no outlet, no channel. His eyes were glassy. His lips were chapped and bee-stung.

"Teancum Mahonri Leon, I love you more than I've ever loved anyone, but if you don't fuck me right now, I'm going to kill you."

Jem made another of those choked noises when Tean entered him, and Tean stilled them both, one hand slick on Jem's hip. Jem's eyes were closed. His face and neck and chest mottled with a flush. He nodded. When Tean didn't move, Jem bucked up into him and whimpered.

Tean made it last as long as he could, but it wasn't long enough. He was starved for this, hadn't known he was starving for it, and that need battled with the desire to make it perfect for Jem. Jem's eyes opened, but only partway, hooded with desire. He looked drunk. He came with Tean's hand around him, crying out wordlessly, and a few moments later Tean stuttered through his own orgasm.

They lay together, Jem's arm around him, and the starlight made their sweat glisten. Tean kissed Jem's shoulder, and Jem let out a giggle.

"You're not supposed to laugh," Tean said, poking him in the side. "You're going to give me a complex. Another complex, I mean."

"You're too good. It's unnatural. You're just too fucking good at that."

"You always make it good for me."

"Yeah, but—I mean, you are good." He drew out the word.

"You're not just saying that?"

Jem's eyes narrowed, and in the darkness, Tean felt his face heat.

"Hold on," Jem said.

"Well, Ammon never really wanted me to—I mean, I don't have a lot to compare it to. Just that time in Vegas."

"You have no idea how incredible you are." He ran a sticky hand through Tean's hair and kissed his forehead, then his mouth, surprisingly chaste. "And I'm not just talking about how you fucked my brains out. Although, God, I am going to keep you very, very busy this weekend."

"Just this weekend?"

Growling, Jem rolled on top of him and kissed him again, more deeply this time. "Definitely not just this weekend." He brushed his lips against Tean's and whispered, "I love you, Teancum Leon."

"I love you too."

Jem slept first, his breathing evening out, his arm relaxing where he held Tean against him. Tean, though, drifted. Waves of waking and sleeping. The comfort of a warm body, of feeling protected and safe. The tickle of Jem's breath on his neck. The fragrance of Scope, minty clean. Outside, the aspens sang their last song to the mountains, and a coyote called to the moon, and the wildness of wild things was a kind of wildness in Tean's heart. He pulled Jem's hand to his mouth, kissed his knuckles, and then he slept.

About the Author

Learn more about Gregory Ashe and forthcoming works at
www.gregoryashe.com.

For advanced access, exclusive content, limited-time promotions,
and insider information, please sign up for my mailing list at
http://bit.ly/ashemailinglist.

Made in the USA
Monee, IL
22 March 2024

55454111R00052